CHABLIS

AND

THE DILDO FROM HELL

by

J. Wayne Frye

As a young boy I loved watching the 1932 movie classic *Frankenstein* with my mother on the Late Show. It enthralled and captivated me, so herein is a tale based, in a large part, on that exciting book and movie. Of course, I have taken the story and elevated it to an absurd level, or is it really that absurd? Perhaps there is grand profundity in what appears absurd.

CHABLIS AND THE DILDO FROM HELL

TO:
My dear friend Bruce, who gave me the idea for Dandy Dildo

AND AS ALWAYS, TO MY MUSE
Lynton Viñas and to Mary Shelly

Catalogue Number: 2014-2453599

ISBN: 978-1-928183-19-8

Fireside Books – Victoria, British Columbia
Part of the Peninsula Publishing Consortium

J. Wayne Frye

CHABLIS AND THE DILDO FROM HELL

TABLE OF CONTENTS

Prologue - 5
Dildo Mania
Chapter 1 - 9
Your Itch is a Bit Higher Up
Chapter 2 - 25
When You Have Carlton
Chapter 3 - 35
A Gun Spitting Lead
Chapter 4 - 55
The Rest of the Story is a Tragedy
Chapter 5 - 75
Euphoria of Mind, Body and Spirit
Chapter 6 - 91
Angelic Act of Kindness
Chapter 7 - 105
While He Lay There In Pain
Chapter 8 - 127
Godzilla Was a Pussycat
Chapter 9 - 147
The Dildo from Hell
Chapter 10 - 157
Hell Hath no Fury like that of a Dildo Scorned
Chapter 11 - 175
It Will Destroy You
Chapter 12 - 189
The Last Impediment Had Died
Epilogue - 197
The Light of Hope Flickered

CHABLIS AND THE DILDO FROM HELL

ABOUT THE AUTHOR

Wayne Frye's *Aaron Adams* mysteries, *Chablis Louise Chavez* thrillers, *Girl* books and *Lynton* adventures titillate the brains of those who enjoy tantalizing tales. His life, like the heroes he writes about, has been filled with adventure and excitement.

He has been a college hockey coach, professor, and at one time, the youngest university president in the USA. Called a marketing genius by the *Los Angeles Times*, he has been a promotional consultant to hockey teams and motion picture companies. He has been cited for his work with inner-city gangs in Los Angeles and is active in the anti-globalization movement. A proud Canadian, he divides his time between Ladysmith, British Columbia; Laguna, Philippines and Cape Town, South Africa. He provides satirical political commentary to many Canadian newspapers.

Some of the 44 books by J. Wayne Frye

White Meteors and the Ghost of Sue Ann McGee
Hockey Mania and the Mystery of Nancy Running Elk
Something Evil in the Darkness at Hopkins House
How Hockey Saved a Jew From the Holocaust
The Girl Who Stirred up the Whirlwind
The Girl Who Motivated Murder Most Foul
The Girl Who Said Goodbye for the Last Time
Sammy Sasquatch and the Sts'ailes Star
Fall From Apocalypse
Armageddon Now
Worth Part 1: Roaring Through life Like a Comet in the Midnight Sky
Worth Part 2: The Night of Thunder Road
When Jesus Came to Jersey as the Son of Thunder
When Jesus Came to Canada to Lead an Indigenous Rebellion
Canadian Angels of Mercy – Nurses in Times of Peril
Points of Rebellion: Aboriginals Who Fought for Justice
Lynton Walks on Water
Lynton Curls Her Hair
Lynton and the Vampire at Tagaytay Manor
Lynton Buys a Cell-Phone and Hears the Voice of Doom
Lynton Viñas and Beowulf Perez in the Taal Inferno
Lynton and the Ghosts in the Mansion on Balete Drive
Lynton Viñas: Shadow in the Darkness
Lynton's South African Adventure
Lynton, the Karoo Vampire and the Jewels of Omar Bin Abi
Lynton and the Stellenbosch Terror
Chablis: Avenging Angel for the Forgotten
In the City of Lost Hope
Chablis and the Terrorist
Pursuit
The Disappearance

J. Wayne Frye

CHABLIS AND THE DILDO FROM HELL

PROLOGUE
DILDO MANIA

OK, those who have read previous Chablis (pronounced Sha-blee) adventures know she is not exactly Mother Teresa when it comes to sexuality. Being a non-operative transsexual, her use of a dildo was one way she kept her anal opening wide, supple and ready for action with her lovers, of whom, she had many. Of course, her preferred method of keeping it open was the real thing being rammed up into her with great fury. However, this particular night she had just finished up a trying case and was alone relaxing.

As she lay naked on the bed, she reached over, pulled out her night stand drawer and removed her favourite toy. It was eight inches long (20.3 centremetres) and five inches (12.7 centremetres) in circumference. She arched her back upward, brought her feet up to her butt and lifted her pelvis off the bed while easing the tip of the dildo into her generous opening. Without hesitation, she shoved it all the way in, letting out a low moan.

Pumping furiously up and down, up and down, she was enjoying the fantastic pounding as she dreamed of a lover's pulsating cock pushing deeper and deeper into her body, ramming her into oblivion. Since the age of 15, when she had seduced the manager of the Mexican factory where she worked by bending over his desk and offering her most intimate part for his pleasure, she had revelled in the grand sensation she got from having a man's member deep inside her. She never had to touch her cock, because the pounding in her ass, the throbbing cock of her lover pumping back and forth was so exhilaratingly sensual that she would cum spontaneously. She suddenly exploded in a fury and collapsed on the dildo which was still buried deep within her. She continued to wiggle and squirm, enjoying the sensation of having her prostrate massaged. As she worked her sphincter muscles, she could feel the dildo sinking deeper and deeper inside her gapping cavity. She began to laugh and think about what she might say when she went to the emergency room and asked the doctor to pull a dildo out of her ass since it had gotten lost inside her massive cavity that devoured cocks like Americans devoured patriotic rhetoric and calls to Jesus. She began to laugh and it felt good as the sensation of the laugh made the dildo tickle her prostrate and suddenly she was ready for another pumping session. She quickly pulled her feet up under her butt again, lifted her pelvis high into the air and grabbing the end of the dildo started another wild ride.

Chablis is probably one of the most sexually liberated people you would ever run across. In fact, she once said of her blow jobs: "Even my worst blow job is more gorgeous than a beautiful sunset, more glorious than a rousing fanfare in a symphony. Simply put, I am the best cock sucker ever born."

As she violently exploded with a heart-pounding second orgasm, she sighed with sensuous delight, lying there in bed with the dildo way up her anal cavity, feeling the blissfulness of sexual merriment. She had been to the mountaintop of pleasure and experienced the incredible grandeur of surveying all that lay ahead of her below in the valley of carnal delights. Hers was a life of complete harmony with her own sexuality, and no pontificating religious paragons of virtue, no moralistic bombastic preachers of banality could ever make her bow before the hypocrisy laden manifests of stupidity that they used to imprison people in the mindless claptrap of manipulation that was used to keep them in constant fear of damnation and hellfire. She had no fear of hell, because she knew that hell was man-made. The real hell was an economic system based on greed that institutionalized poverty, so the rich could live lives of splendorous luxury by exploiting cheap labour.

Some readers may think this vivid sexual description is nothing more than a diversion into titillating sex-oriented literature. However, as this story develops it will become obvious that Chablis' predilection for using dildos when no man was available would actually be a prime catalyst in a case that would be one of the most unusual she ever tackled. After all, as Chablis also said about fornicating, "Sex without love is a meaningless experience, but as far as meaningless experiences go it's pretty damn good."

CHABLIS AND THE DILDO FROM HELL

CHAPTER 1
YOUR ITCH IS A BIT HIGHER UP

The sun was glistening on my bald-pate,
As I strolled toward sin's open gate
For a round of peccadilloes with women of night.
Yet another tête-à-tête in grand delight.
Someone most salacious in her bare skin
Did open the door and let me in.

Upon arriving I was ushered into sin's den
And I saw a grand dildo playing with skin,
So I offered my throbbing pounding piece,
Into the breach I went thrusting in,
And to my joy found no barrier
To diving in that hot wall of skin.

Oh, there were asses galore at the stake,
And pussy there to gloriously take.
I could not believe there was so much,
And I wanted to eat it all for my lunch
My oh my, asses were on an altar,

CHABLIS AND THE DILDO FROM HELL

And believe me, I did not falter.

And I gave myself to pleasure,
And I lost myself in sin,
And I set about my purpose
Of pounding some skin.
But all the time the dildo was there,
And it got more than its fair share.

Was it not prophesied by heathens long ago:
"Within the walls of Sodom, any man may go?"
And as I found myself staring at pussy galore,
I longed for dissolution with yet another whore.
But that damn dildo paraded around,
And many an ass did it pound.

There were so many women wildly on the make,
Wiggling their asses for any man to take.
Still that dildo paraded around
Ass after ass to perversely pound.
They all begged it their asses to break.
They wanted more than any ass could take.

Exhausted, I lay back upon a wooden church pew
And gazed upon the vision of that dildo anew;
To such a deep delight each woman did it win,
As they begged to cram it in.
All the while, the music of the fleshly spheres
Played on the orchestra of their skin.

But as I stood once more prepared
To enter the carnal fray

10   **J. Wayne Frye**

CHABLIS AND THE DILDO FROM HELL

It seemed my libido had nothing to say.
Therein lays the rub my friend.
Only a dildo has the power
To fornicate without any end!

As I detail this unusual case, I shall forestall any discussion of what might be peripheral issues and try to concentrate on the real measure of what occurred that is now sometimes simply referred to as the parade of dildo dalliances of delightful diversions.

Chablis had corresponded through e-mail with a woman who had later died, and each morning she got up to check her e-mail and found that she was forlorn as she had always looked forward to hearing from her friend Celeste every day. She bowed her head and thought about how they had enjoyed each others company, even often sharing wild tales of fornication with men they found particularly blessed with sexual prowess. There had been much laughter between the two and they had often joked about a good dildo being a poor substitute for a man, but a sometimes necessary evil. Chablis got a smile on her face as she remembered the previous night's use of a dildo to bring her pleasure and relax her for a good night's sleep. In fact, so overcome with carnal thoughts of the pleasure from the previous night, she sighed deeply and looked down at her naked body and began to gently stroke it with both hands. The warmth of it filled her with deep satisfaction.

CHABLIS AND THE DILDO FROM HELL

She got up, went to her bedroom and brought out the trusty toy that had delivered her so much pleasure the night before. She lay down on the bed, and placing the dildo beside her, she began to massage her perky little hormone developed breasts that were perfectly symmetrical and had cute pointed nipples that seemed to beg to be sucked. Closing her eyes and imaging a viral lover performing that task, she slowly moved her right hand downward until arriving at her right hip. She thrust her pelvis upward and eased her right hand onto her crack and began to rub gently and felt a wave of exhilaration as she touched with her middle finger the opening to the gates of paradise for so many. It slid in easily and she began to move it around the opening, moaning as she reached over and took the dildo with her left hand, brought it under her butt, removed her finger and began to tantalizingly tease her love canal as she gently and methodically guided it into the opening. As she pressed against her sphincter muscle it almost completely collapsed as it gobbled up the device like a person who had not eaten in a week and had just had a huge banquet laid before them. Damn, she loved being filled up with a love tool. She began to push it deeper and deeper until the top of her fingers were also inside her as she started pumping furiously back and forth, back and forth. She would bring it almost completely out and then shove it in deep and hard. She began to thrust her perfectly shaped hips upward to meet each downward motion.

J. Wayne Frye

CHABLIS AND THE DILDO FROM HELL

Before long she exploded her milky white substance all over her belly and let out a mighty guttural proclamation of delicious satisfaction. She lay there for awhile enjoying the magnificence of the moment and vowed she would soon get the real thing rammed into her so she could experience true euphoria that could only be offered by a man.

In Manhattan, a large income is in the millions, not hundreds of thousands and certainly Aaron Adams and Chablis Louise Chavez, although running a successful detective agency, were not in that category. They inhabited walk-up condos in lower Manhattan and their office was on the Upper East Side, but far from the high rent district.

Chablis was a beautiful brown skinned Mexican immigrant, who, as a transsexual, faced many prejudicial obstacles in a nation filled with judgmental religious bigoted hypocrites who spent an inordinate amount of time pointing the finger of damnation rather than embracing people with compassion. Chablis had never had much use for religion since being fondled by the village priest who was always ogling her tiny breasts and trying to fornicate with her while publicly condemning her for wearing dresses and acting like a girl. According to him, God did not make mistakes and she was a boy and should act like one. She once told him, "You are a priest. Why don't you act like one?" Many years later she would laugh upon looking back at his lechery and answer her own question – "he was acting like one." Hypocrites filled the pews of most churches, which was why she avoided them like a plague.

She and Aaron had made love once and they both deemed it a mistake as partners should avoid romantic entanglements. It never happened again, but they did enjoy each others company, so they often took vacations together, even sharing the same room on occasion, but never the same bed. So, it was in late October that they made a trip to Vermont where they got separate rooms in the Algonquin Resort outside Brattleboro to enjoy a few days rest. The rest was to be short-lived.

Here in this isolated place, where everything is so marvelously cheap, they really enjoyed all the luxuries and comforts at an affordable price. It was at the hotel where Chablis met Carlton Broughton in the lounge. He was a relatively rich middle aged man who had an estate in the nearby mountains. He called it his feudal estate as it gave the appearance of being a castle. Inviting Chablis was for an obvious reason, so she felt compelled to tell him that he might be disappointed as she was a pre-op transgender girl. Being an educated man, he shrugged his shoulders and said, "I know all about gender dysphasia, so I would not be shocked. Anyway, who said anything about inviting you for sex?"

CHABLIS AND THE DILDO FROM HELL

Laughing, Chablis replied "Well, I am always prepared for the eventuality when a man is involved. In fact, even women are sometimes as bad as men when it comes to sex."

"You are a beautiful woman Chablis," he said with a note of deep sincerity in his voice, and continued, "Any man would be a fool not to try, but that is not the reason I am inviting you."

"Then, I accept, but only if you promise to try."

Laughing, he replied, "Believe me, I will try."

"Well, there is one other thing. I am up here with my partner. You have probably heard of him."

Nodded his head affirmatively, he said "Of course I know of him. Who doesn't? You and he are famous thanks to the writer, Wayne Frye."

"Don't believe everything you read."

"Well, Dr. Frye says you are beautiful in his books, and I certainly can believe that."

Smiling, she added, "Well, Wayne is certainly a weaver of fine tales, and as you know, writers do embellish. Would Aaron also be invited?

"Oh, he is invited too, of course."

CHABLIS AND THE DILDO FROM HELL

"Grand, I shall tell him, and we will be there in the morning. Does that suit you?"

"Well, tonight would be better. What do you say?"

"Done."

Nothing can be more picturesque or solitary than the place Carlton Broughton called home. It stood in grand eminence in a forest. The road, very old and narrow, passed in front of it and the place, built like a castle was surrounded by an actual moat with a drawbridge. The moat was filled with fish and inhabited by huge swans, and floating on its surface were white fleets of water lilies.

Over all this the castle showed its many-windowed front; its towers, and its Gothic steeple. The forest opened in an irregular and very picturesque glade before its gate, and at the right a bridge carried the road over a stream that wound in deep shadow through the woods. It was such a very lonely place that Chablis and Aaron felt a chill. From the front of the gigantic building looking towards the road, the forest in which the castle stood extended many kilometres to the right and left. The nearest village was about seven kilometres to the left. The nearest inhabited place with any population was Brattleboro where slightly over 12,000 people lived, but it was as if that place was a thousand kilometers away.

CHABLIS AND THE DILDO FROM HELL

Only three kilometres westward, in the direction toward Brattleboro, a ruined village, with its quaint little church, now roofless, in the aisle of which are the mouldering tombs of a local family of grand legend called the Karsons, now extinct, who once owned the equally desolate chateau there, which, in the thick of the forest, overlooks the silent ruins of the deserted village. At a later date, the story behind the desertion of this striking and melancholy spot shall be detailed.

The castle was attended by a handful of servants who seemed reticent to engage in conversation. Carlton's father was stern looking, but still a kind appearing man who seemed to be hobbled by old age as he scooted around with apparent difficulty. No doubt, he was well into his late seventies as Carlton appeared to be in his fifties. It was indeed unusual in the USA, where the best health care is reserved for the wealthy, to see someone with this much wealth in ill health at almost any age. The last remnant of for-profit healthcare in the First World, the USA was looked upon as an abomination by both Chablis and Aaron who believed healthcare was a right not a privilege.

Carlton and his father constituted what was left of the family at the castle. Mrs. Broughton had died in Carlton's infancy, but he had a good-natured governess, who had been with him so long that she was almost like a mother to him. She was fat, maybe 65 and appeared a kindly lady.

CHABLIS AND THE DILDO FROM HELL

They learned the governess, Miss Diane Rhoades, who now seemed to just live there with no apparent function, was a native of Romania, whose care and good nature assuaged Carlton's loss of his mother at around 7. You could sense he deeply revered his mother by the tone of his voice when he mentioned her.

There was also a sixth at the dinner table, a Miss Ione Lawson, an elegant looking lady of maybe 35, who was simply introduced as head of the household, which apparently meant she was the head maid. She spoke fluent Spanish, which endeared her to Chablis who enjoyed using her native language.

These were regular social resources according to Carlton, but the isolation made visitors an infrequent affair. However, there were regular visits to the nearest neighbours. Yet, for the most part, the people there lived pretty much like hermits. In fact, Carlton complained that his life was primarily solitary one which is why he was so anxious to invite his two famous guests.

Carlton admitted to being a bit spoiled by all the people in the household ever since he was a child. All at the dinner party readily agreed that they often humoured him with lavish attention. Chablis mentioned that she felt the same way about Aaron, as she had to baby him like a father spoiled by an adoring daughter.

J. Wayne Frye

CHABLIS AND THE DILDO FROM HELL

Aaron offered a cogent rejoinder; "Yeah, and like I don't spoil her."

After dinner, Mr. Broughton excused himself for an early bedtime and the two ladies also retired for the evening, leaving Aaron, Chablis and Carlton sitting by the gigantic fireplace in the living room. It was there that Carlton began to share intimate details of his life, and also to perhaps reveal the real reason he wanted his two famous guests there.

As they sat by the fire in the huge study to which they had retired, Carlton turned to his two guests in earnest and said, "I know you two are open-minded and embrace diversity. I am also sure you both have a healthy attitude toward sex, so please don't think me crude with what I am about to discuss, and be assured that you have never encountered any tale as wild and fanciful as what I am about to share.

Aaron said, "Don't be so sure of that. We have encountered some pretty wild things."

"Ah, but this is one so fantastic, so incredible that I sometimes can't believe it myself. You see, there is a legend connected to the Karson family. You have seen the ruins of their ancestral home near here.

Chablis interjected, "Yes, we have and a very foreboding and eerie looking place it is."

CHABLIS AND THE DILDO FROM HELL

"First of all, please don't consider me offensive, but I am about to spin a tale that will seem impossible, and it involves sexuality carried to the extreme. You see, the Karson family was obsessed with sexuality, and there were even rumours of incest within the family. That being said, let me be as tactful as possible while explaining the problem as I see it."

Chablis actually felt a little tingle between her legs and her sphincter muscle seemed to relax as she became, as usual when sex was mentioned, highly titillated. She leaned slightly forward and said, "Do not worry about being tactful. Tell the story as explicitly as possible so that we know exactly what we are dealing with. Based upon our past experiences, we are well-beyond being shocked by almost any revelation."

Carlton sighed, leaned back in the large overstuffed chair and began. "The Karson family lived here for over 500 years and they were a somewhat eccentric lot. Around 1900, the patriarch was James Karson, and he was a renowned inventor, holding many patents on various things. He was in his 60's and had married a young woman of only 20. Now, as one might expect, it was assumed that the young woman in question married for money. After many years that contention is not settled, but perhaps it is irrelevant anyway, as the real interesting thing about the marriage was the rumours that she was a

J. Wayne Frye

dominant who catered to James Karson's desires to be made into a wimp who loved to be forced to worship her on his knees with his tongue filling every nook, corner and crevice she had. Now, Karson, as I said was an inventor, and what he set out to invent will probably make you laugh, but as he aged he could no longer get an erection, so his wife kept insisting she needed a big love muscle in her as often as possible. Now, his love for the woman was almost unfathomable. In the early 1900's they had dildos, but no battery operated vibrators. Karson set his genius for invention in motion to develop the ultimate dildo for his wife, one that would bring her the most incredible orgasms imaginable. He was working in his laboratory day and night with great devotion to the cause. It actually became an overriding obsession with him."

At this point, Aaron and Chablis were both fighting back laughter, as they had tackled many cases, but this one was about to top them all for eccentricity and pure top of the gauge on the laugh metre. Carlton looked at them, and realizing they were holding back laughter, said "Go ahead, laugh. It is O.K."

As they both burst out in laughter, he joined them and the joviality became so resounding that they all practically bent over from the intensity of their jocularity. After a few minutes, they all settled down and Chablis said, "O.K., I think we have ourselves under control now. Please go ahead, if you are indeed serious."

Without cracking a smile, he said "Oh, I am serious, so serious that I look upon what I am about to reveal to you as the horror of all horrors. It is, in reality, not a tale for the faint of heart."

Chablis began to think of an old poem she had read many years ago:
.

> *Fill your head with false bravado*
> *Dance about incognito*
> *Breath like rotted avocado*
> *You say tomato,*
> *I say tomahto*
> *Set your dildo on vibrator*
> *And go fuck yourself*

Again, she burst out in nearly uncontrollable laughter until the two men asked her to please share the fun with them. She recited the poem and they all again laughed in unison until Aaron finally said, "Carlton, we are sorry. Please continue with you story and we shall try to contain our frivolous nature in regards to what you are sharing."

"It is O.K. I understand, and I don't expect you to even believe all I am revealing, but this is a genuine tale of what will, no doubt, be the most fantastic of all the cases you have tackled in all your years of detecting. Be patient and I shall reveal the most incredible tale you have ever heard."

Aaron and Chablis vowed to themselves to restrain their laughter so Carlton could tell his story about Daniel Karson's vow to invent the ultimate dildo. "O.K., so as he worked diligently to put this master invention together, and his wife began to anticipate with glee her coming euphoric rendezvous with the invention that they were now calling Mr. Dandy Dildo. Word spread far and wide in the area about the man's singular devotion to the cause of erotic stimulation. People would drive their horse and buggies by day and night and they would always see the lights on in the laboratory as Karson simply lived his life entirely for the completion of his invention. Meantime, his son Darryl became so worried about him that he called in a local doctor who treated him for exhaustion."

Carlton took a sip of wine and continued. "Karson was like Dr. Frankenstein, he believed he was creating something with a life force in it that would bring his dear wife the ultimate orgasm. In fact, he, like Dr. Frankenstein, became literally obsessed with the notion that he was creating a life force like no other. It would be the ultimate in erotic stimulation and he would implant a brain in it so that it could understand the needs and desires of the women it would serve. Yes, he was about to make men as lovers obsolete. Once a woman had experienced Dandy Dildo, nothing else would ever satisfy her."

Suddenly, Aaron's cell rang and he was being summoned back to New York City immediately to help a client they had been working with for several weeks. He had to excuse himself and assured Carlton that Chablis was well-up to any task that was required to solve a case that had not even been completely laid out yet. Chablis walked him to the door and said, "Hey, you know you're right."

Aaron, perplexed said, "Right about what?"

"Right about me being able to handle anything that comes up." She winked as she said it, because she was an expert at handling erections. They laughed and Aaron knew she was indeed up to handling anything that came up between a man's legs. She was a woman who would never be satisfied with just a dildo, as she got too much pleasure from her oral pursuits. He kissed her on the cheek and said, "Dildos are dandy manifestations that can scratch an itch between a woman's legs or lower cheeks, but your itch is a bit higher up."

CHAPTER 2
WHEN YOU HAVE CARLTON

You ladies of merry old Vermont
Who have had erotic delight nibble your hand,
Did you not lately see Karson's sex show,
And a noble thing called Dandy Dildo?

This stiff member was on an erotic train
And helps to conduct you over the main;
But now it is said he must go,
You have had your fill of Dandy Dildo.

At the sign of tingling on erotic street,
When you go thither to make yourselves sweet
By buying of powder, make-up, essence, or so,
You may by chance play with Dandy Dildo.

You would take him at first for no person of note,
Because he appears in a plain rubber coat,
But when you his sensual abilities know,
You'll fall down and worship Dandy Dildo.

J. Wayne Frye   25

CHABLIS AND THE DILDO FROM HELL

One lady I know, tingled her sexual fort
Clothed him in satin, then brought him to court;
But his head in the circle he scarcely did show,
This thick and stiff rubber Dandy Dildo.

The good lady, thinking no harm,
Had this poor stiff thing hid under her arm.
This lady's daughter came the secret to know,
And from her own mother stole Dandy Dildo.

A countess of whom people tell
Eyes the stiffness and soon fell.
How she grabbed it all in the know
Wanting the lusty swinger Dandy Dildo.

By the help of this gallant thick and long waif
Against the fierce desire preserved herself safe;
She put him lovingly beneath her pillow,
So closely she embraced Dandy Dildo.

The pattern of virtue was nowhere in the land.
Women shoved him in like shifting sand;
Rubbing and scrubbing so wide does it grow.
Oh the women learned to love Dandy Dildo.

A dainty fine duchess loved this fine trick.
She doted on it as nature's finest prick,
Oh, all its fierceness she came to know
The grandiose vigour of Dandy Dildo.

A duchess though she looked high,
On the fine thing came to rely,

J. Wayne Frye

CHABLIS AND THE DILDO FROM HELL

For fear her secrets they should know,
For her gentleman friend was Dandy Dildo.

Another countess – what's her name?
She was a famous sex loving dame.
When her old lovers forsook her, where'd she go?
Where else but to Dandy Dildo?

When tired of Vermont, the rubber stood tall
And headed south for other women to ball.
Oh, how the women pleaded with it not to go.
They desperately needed Dandy Dildo.

Old men could no longer roam their wife's range,
And therefore some actually offered an exchange:
They knew that only one thing was wanted below.
The women needed to be rammed by Dandy Dildo.

Women with wrinkles and lines on each face,
Had reserved for it a very special place.
Yes they needed it so bad, why did it go?
They needed ramming with Dandy Dildo.

This fine stiffness was a grand cop,
All the wives their holes to mop.
Oh, how his legend did grow and grow
Even the Pope soon learned of Dandy Dildo.

The town mayor's wife, that fine flower,
At the sight of it did faint and belch sour,
And her good breeding upon his return did show.
Bowing she said, "Welcome home Dandy Dildo.

J. Wayne Frye   27

CHABLIS AND THE DILDO FROM HELL

He civilly came to grind her good one night,
And proffered his service to all within sight.
"Umm" she said with it deep in her back hole.
"You are so very, very good Dandy Dildo."

Thus it was sound, safe, ready to give her some.
It was better than candle, carrot, or thumb;
Throw away those nasty devices, and show
How you rate the just merit of Dandy Dildo.

Count Cazzo, who carried his nose very high,
In passion he swore his rival should die;
Then shut himself up to let the world know
Flesh and blood could not defeat Dandy Dildo.

A rabble of pricks who were welcome before,
Now finding the porter denied them the door,
Maliciously waited his coming below
And inhumanly fell on Dandy Dildo.

Nigh worn out, still it did fly,
And along the promenade the women did cry;
They bellowed and whined from every window,
Shouting, "For heaven's sake, save Dandy Dildo."

The good ladies soon had no laughter.
They were forlorn and all wobbling after.
And each husband was now their determined foe,
All the hard-ons disappeared with Dandy Dildo.

Having read the poem to Chablis written by a
local husband who was thrilled that the evil of the

J. Wayne Frye

CHABLIS AND THE DILDO FROM HELL

Karson invented dildo was gone, he looked at her and said, "So, basically that is the story. The dildo invented by Karson laid waste to the men in the community as women had no need for them other than as procreators. Now, what the dildo truly did to so enthral women no one knows today. In fact, few know the story, and the few who know the story either do not believe or do not know what the magical hold over women was. Truth is, Karson and his wife died shortly after he invented the damn thing, and some think that he retrieved it so that she could live happily with it to satisfy her carnal desires as she awaited death."

Chablis bowed her head, kept it lowered for awhile and said. "OK, so it is a funny story, and you have certainly entertained me, but what is the point? What am I or Aaron supposed to do in regards to this fantastic tale? I mean we are detectives, so where's the rub here my dear Carlton."

"Oh, I simply want you to find this thing. Hey, I do not believe the whole story, but I do believe there is money to be made if it can be located and the story told. My guess is the value would be well over a million dollars. You may think living here we are rich, but we struggle to pay the taxes on this monstrosity every year. My father is old and this is the only home he has ever known. I do not want him to die any other place but here. I want him to end his days in the place he loves."

CHABLIS AND THE DILDO FROM HELL

Chablis, still mystified and baffled, said "OK, we get $1000 a day plus expenses. We aren't cheap, but if you want me to look into this ridiculous story it is your money and I'll take the case. I assume I can stay here?"

"I wish you would, yes."

Chablis could feel the sensuous nature of his comment and knew exactly what he was hinting at. "Well, I do like a relaxing round of sex before going to sleep, so maybe I will need a dildo. Do you have any?"

He got up, went over and standing before her as she looked up longingly at him, said "No, but I can furnish something almost as good."

Smiling, Chablis began to unzip his pants as she said, "For my desires, this is much better."

She gently lowered his pants and his monstrous erection made her sigh as she realized she was about to devour a beautiful member that was long, thick and cut. She wrapped her hands around his butt and pulled him toward her as she took his monster meat into her mouth in one smooth gulp. She prided herself on never seeing a joy stick that she could not swallow with precision. She was an expert and she knew it. She gracefully worked her mouth back and forth on his root of passion as he moaned with delight.

CHABLIS AND THE DILDO FROM HELL

Carlton's ecstasy was apparent as he let Chablis feast on his meat as he steadfastly fed it to her willingly warm mouth. She sucked hard on the tip and pressed the point of her tongue into that cluster of nerves under the head. Forcing her face down all the way to his pelvis, she took the full length without a gag reflex and was proud of herself when she sucked like a high-powered commercial vacuum cleaner sweeping up with gusto everything in its path. Carlton seemed to appreciate her efforts as he strained to push himself farther and farther into her moist mouth, making small groans and grunts to confirm her supreme efforts to coax that joy juice she craved from that pulsating scrumptious stick of tasty meat.

She built a slow rhythm and she started grunting herself, as she kept up a furious pace. After maybe 10 minutes of worshipping his member, he started humping into her mouth and she knew he was getting close. It excited her so much that she redoubled her efforts to please him.

Suddenly he spoke more aggressively, "Swallow my load baby, eat it up, gobble up my cum."

He started groaning and shaking as there was a grand spasm and he spurted into her eager mouth. Maybe six or seven mighty squirts of heavy volume sprays volleyed into her throat and she savoured every drop. She let him enjoy the pleasure she was giving him. She didn't want to interrupt his throes of passion by pulling off, as she swallowed gulp after gulp from his pulsating pole of pure delight. After he was drained dry, she let him rest it in her mouth and go soft, which made her realize grand euphoria as she prided herself on her oral prowess with men of all shapes and sizes.

Collapsing on the sofa beside her, he put his arms around her as she snuggled up to him and said, "Now, I expect you to share my bed tonight and get rejuvenated soon so you can fill my hole of pleasure with that monster meat. The opening is quivering now in anticipation."

At that, he rose, removed his clothes, reached down and pulled her pants off. Her own member popped to attention as he turned her over, and removed her panties as she grabbed the back of the sofa. He reached down, spread her beautiful ass cheeks and he began to nuzzle his face between them. He teased the hole with his tongue, kissed it, sucked on it and felt the opening completely relax. Suddenly, the titillation made his member spring to life. He was rock hard and ready to take the mighty plunge into paradise. Chablis jutted her ass out, relaxed her cheeks exposing that little brown hole that was quivering with anticipation of a resounding pounding that would make her think she was a car engine with pistons ramming rapidly up and down firing on all cylinders, and it was not a V-4 or a V-6. It was a V-8 roaring at maximum capacity.

So furious was Carlton's thrusts that Chablis thought a couple of times he was going to slam her so hard and so deep that she would actually go through the back of the sofa. The ride was wild, uninhibited and furious with the final explosion coming like a volcano blowing its top. The explosion rocked her so hard that her member spurted cum all over the back of the sofa as she came spontaneously without manipulating her small pole at all. She let out a slow satisfied moan as Carlton stayed buried all the way up her shaft of golden delight that he had mined with his mighty prick. As he went soft, he bent over and kissed her on the neck, whispering, "You are the most incredible woman I have ever met Chablis."

Letting out a satisfied laugh she said, "I always get like this when I hear wild dildo tales."

They laughed on the way upstairs, holding hands, crawled into Carlton's bed and spent the night wrapped in each others arms. The following morning led to another fantastic blow job for Carlton and another pounding for Chablis. They would both start their day exhilarated and happy.

The old man and the two ladies who joined them for breakfast could not hide their prurient interest, as they had no doubt heard the wild fornicating the previous night and morning. Chablis looked over at Carlton's father and gave him a little wink just to let him know he should be proud of his son.

They smiled at each other and Chablis prepared for her first day on the case of the Dandy Dildo. She thought "Who needs a dildo when you have Carlton?"

.

CHAPTER 3
A GUN SPITTING LEAD

I know what you are thinking
And you may be right
That thing that vibrates
Brings such delight

There are different sizes
Some in colours too
Means you don't need a man
'Cause double "A" batteries will do

Anytime you want
Anytime you ask
A dildo can provide you
And gloriously complete the task

You can shut it off
Put it in a drawer
Try doing that with a man
Just another option to explore

J. Wayne Frye   35

CHABLIS AND THE DILDO FROM HELL

The first thing on Chablis' agenda, as in every case she undertook, was to get all the background information she could. She went into the study where Carlton's father was sitting in an overstuffed recliner with a book in his hand. At 82, he was still a very nice looking gentleman with thick grey hair that slightly grazed the top of his ears and was meticulously swept toward the back of his head. His medium length hair wafted around him like a gentle cloud fluffily curling and moving of its own volition. His eyes twinkled with that bit of wisdom that comes with age. You instinctively knew this was a man who had lived life with gusto, and even in old age there was still that hint of devil-may-care desire to be a lover of women who could masterfully make them swoon. Chablis strangely felt herself attracted to him, if for no other reason, because he was so gentlemanly and oozed with sophistication that was not overbearing but confident. You just knew this was a man of quality.

Motioning for her to sit down, Chablis took a seat immediately in front of him by the fireplace. He smiled at her and said, "You have been hired by my son to find that contraption invented for pleasure. Yet, you have your doubts that it ever existed. Based upon what I heard last night, you enjoy the real thing better than the fake."

Smiling broadly, Chablis replied, "Well, I hope we did not disturb your sleep."

CHABLIS AND THE DILDO FROM HELL

Nodding his head left to right and letting a grin crease his lips, he replied, "Quiet the contrary. It gave me such a dandy erection. I called Ione into my chamber. That is, in fact, why I keep her on; she finds old men appealing, and at my age, I find all women appealing if they give me an opportunity to exercise what little I have left of a libido. When a man is too old to dream of fornication, he might as well lie down and let them shovel the earth over him."

Smiling, Chablis offered a cogent observation. "I am sure, from what I see that you are a man who never had any problems attracting women."

You could see the pride swelling up in him as he placed the book he had on the table beside him and said, "Well, I was a bit too free with my libido I am afraid. Unrestrained debauchery is grand fun, but it cost me in the long run I suppose. My wife was never replaced in my mind, of course."

Wanting to massage an old man's ego, Chablis chortled, "Well, you just can't corral a wild mustang."

They laughed together as he scratched his beautiful hair and said, "You flatter an old man. You, my dear, are a lady who knows how to manipulate men. Touché!"

"I have a feeling nobody manipulates you."

CHABLIS AND THE DILDO FROM HELL

"You are an astute observer of the human psyche."

"I am a trained detective, and I graduated at the top of my class."

"That I can believe. So, my son has told you about the famous Dandy Dildo and you want to pick my brain."

"Well, no offence, but it has been close to 100 years since Karson invented the little, excuse me, the big titillating machine of fanciful fornicating for women; consequently, I assume the older generation might have heard some stories about this tickler of women's honey pots. Perhaps you can recall something that might be of assistance."

He got up, went over to a bookshelf, removed a small dusty old book and blew the dust off it. He walked over and handed it to her. "If you and my son had spent more time studying the history of Dandy Dildo than engaging in hanky-panky, perhaps you could have had this knowledge earlier."

Giving him a mischievous look and tilting her head slightly to the side she said, "Hey, life without a bit of hanky-panky would be pretty boring." Then she looked down at the book that said, *Historical Review of Chameleon Village* and continued. "This book has something about Dandy

CHABLIS AND THE DILDO FROM HELL

Dildo?

"Turn to page 78."

Mr. Broughton walked back to his chair and eased himself down as he said, "Go ahead, read it aloud."

Chablis began reading the section headlined Mysterious Occurrences at the Karson Estate in Chameleon Village. *In the year of our Lord 1912, James Karson, aged 66, married a young woman named Kandy Kane (assumed to be her stage name), who was a striptease artist, aged 20. They appeared happy in every way, but there were problems experienced by Mr. Karson in his conjugal duties. It was rumoured that they engaged in SM and BD play in order to facilitate their sexual desires. However, Kandy was young and loved the thrill of fornication on what might be termed a more normal basis. Being totally devoted to Mr. Karson she refused to engage in any extramarital affairs to facilitate her intense desire for penetration by a penis. For that reason, in 1914, her husband, a well-known inventor, set out to develop the ultimate dildo that would bring complete and total satisfaction to the woman he loved. Now, he intended for this to be more than just a dildo. He wanted it to have feelings that would emanate from within and cause the woman to feel as if she was experiencing love making from an item with true erotic feeling.*

CHABLIS AND THE DILDO FROM HELL

Again, Chablis was fighting back laughter, and Mr. Broughton could tell she was trying to restrain herself. He said, "Go ahead Chablis, laugh all you want. I understand."

Suddenly she burst out in laughter and Mr. Broughton could not help but join her. Together they chortled for a good minute before the laughter subsided. Chablis said, "I'm so sorry, Mr. Broughton."

"Don't worry, and James, please."

"O.K. James, should I go on then?"

"Please do."

"O.K. where was I now. Oh, yes, so, *he sat about to create the ultimate in female satisfaction. In fact he became obsessed. This obsession seemed to completely overtake him to the point that he even began to sleep in his laboratory and strange things starting happing in the village.*" She looked up and noticed that James had drifted off to sleep so she began to read to herself. What follows is the entire story according to Karson.

It was on a dreary night of November that I contemplated my decision to develop the perfect dildo for my dear wife. With an anxiety that almost amounted to agony, I collected the instruments of life around me that I might infuse a spark of being into a lifeless thing that would eventually lay on my laboratory table. You see, I wanted the perfect dildo, not from just rubber, plastic or any other substance but the real life flesh of a cadaver. This dildo was an obsession because, as an elderly man, I seemed unable to satisfy my young wife's insatiable desire for a good pounding three or four times a day. You see, despite our enormous age difference, she was truly in love with me, so even when I suggested she find a younger, more virile man to visit her on occasion she simply refused to entertain the notion, saying that her love was reserved for one real man and she simply could not think about meeting anyone else even if it was just for sex.

I must admit to great shame in how I went about fashioning this dildo, but I was simply a man possessed with love for my wife and believed that providing her with a companion for her carnal satisfaction was an act of love. I was a man truly dedicated to a noble cause. I used my faithful servant Harold to collect the parts I needed. First, I wanted the absolute best penis I could possibly find. One that was circumcised of course and one that had at least a minimum of ten inches (25 centremetres) and a circumference of six inches (15 centremetres). I instructed Harold to go to the morgue in nearby Brattleboro and bribe the attendant in order that he might cut off a very nice size penis for me to use.

CHABLIS AND THE DILDO FROM HELL

Unfortunately, without my knowledge, Harold had decided that a truly gargantuan penis would be best, and being a loyal servant, he went to nearby Boston where he prowled the streets finding homosexual men to have sex with in search of the perfect specimen. I later found out that he was performing oral sex on a variety of men in order to ascertain their virility. He was so sensitive that he did not want to hurt these men's feelings by saying their penises were too small for him to engage in sex. Truly devoted and also a man with a heart of gold when it came to hurting someone's feelings he was indeed a man dedicated to his mission.

At this point Chablis put down the book and again fought back laughter, making sure not to laugh out loud for fear of disturbing Mr. Broughton, who was in deep slumber in the easy chair. She looked around the room and asked herself whether the writer of the tryst was being serious or facetious. Surely, he had enough intelligence to know that Harold was simply a closet homosexual who was using Mr. Karson's request as an excuse to engage in said acts at a time when homosexuality was actually a crime. She reached down, picked up the book and continued to read.

So fully devoted to me and the cause I was undertaking, Harold even began to allow men to have anal sex with him because he wanted to find

J. Wayne Frye

the absolute perfect penis that could deliver the ultimate satisfaction to a woman's vagina. What a wonderful man to make such grand sacrifices so that I could help mankind with my invention. Harold came to me and told me what he was doing, but I reminded him that a live penis was impossible to use, so we needed one from a cadaver. It was then when he said, "Mr. Karson, a fresh penis would be so much better."

I thought long and hard, no pun intended, and realized what he was proposing. I looked at him in revulsion and said, "Absolutely not. No way are we killing anyone."

Then he pointed to a picture of my wife that I kept in the laboratory. I hung my head in shame as I whispered, "Yes, a fresh piece of meat would be the best way to bring the dildo to life." To my undying shame, I was at that moment committed to murder in order to perfect the perfect dildo. As a man of science, I was honour bound to bring to life what the world truly needed – a dildo that would be an instrument of grand and glorious satisfaction for all women.

Again, Chablis put the book down, got up and went into the hall where she burst out in laughter. Surely, this whole thing was a giant hoax she thought. She got on her cell and called Aaron. Through laughter, she said, "I don't believe this Aaron. This is like some Frankenstein nightmare."

CHABLIS AND THE DILDO FROM HELL

She then proceeded to relate to him what she had read as they shared uproarious laughter. All Aaron said was that for a thousand dollars a day she should simply humour the guys and have fun.

Chablis said, "O.K., I'll stick it out for a few days simply because I am getting some great sex as part of the deal."

She hung up and walked back into the study, slowly eased down into the chair and began to read again. Karson's words were truly serious with no tinge of frivolity, but Chablis simply could not retrain her laughter and kept her giggles as quiet as possible.

My loyal servant, so devoted to my cause, rented a small apartment in the Soho district where he took men regularly in his search of the perfect penis. I felt so sorry for him having to constantly be sucking and giving up his buttock for poundings from total strangers for the glory of invention. He was truly a man totally devoted to the cause of science.

Then, in early January of the New Year, he came across a man who was packing a full 14 inches (35.5 centremetres) with a circumference of 9 inches (23 centremetres). I suggested he lure him back to our laboratory with the promise of a weekend in sexual bliss so that we might slay him and cut off that magnificent member that seemed

J. Wayne Frye

perfect for my purposes. He hardily agreed and brought the man for a weekend.

Insisting that the man should have one last night of mind blowing sex, my devoted man servant spent the night wildly fornicating with the man with the giant penis. I thought how noble of my servant to do this for the man who was going to donate his penis and his life to the cause of science.

The next morning he brought him into the laboratory and as I was showing him a beaker filled with animal penis specimens, my man servant clubbed him over the head. Instantly placing him on the examining table, we stripped him and I was astonished at the near perfection of his grand penis. Oh, it was a beautiful thing to behold. And what an incredible set of testicles. They reminded me of bowling balls they were so large. Yes, I had to have those too and the nice amount of pubic hair was so wonderful. I thought about how wonderful it would feel for my beloved wife to fondle the balls and feel a surge of passion. I cut with the precision of a skilled surgeon, preserving that magnificent specimen completely intact. I was now beginning to see the light at the end of the proverbial tunnel. Yes, I was about to bring life to a grand and glorious dildo that would forever seal my place in the scientific hall of fame, for I had already perfected a serum to keep the flesh pulsating with life. Oh, I was euphoric.

CHABLIS AND THE DILDO FROM HELL

As my man servant looked down upon the dildo, he said "Oh, it is so dandy."

I was stricken with the perceptiveness of Harold. Yes, it was a dandy dildo indeed. What a name for my great invention – Dandy Dildo. Still, as I looked down upon it there pulsating with life, I knew it needed more. I thought it must have the ability to ejaculate so women could feel the pulsating vibrations that lifted their spirits knowing they stimulated a man to orgasm. Day and night I worked diligently to come up with a way to make it spurt that joyous euphoric elixir. Finally, I realized that a perpetual motion machine implanted within it would keep the cycle of semen production going for eternity. Yes, I would plant the initial semen and the inner workings of the machine would keep harvesting more and more bringing it forever forward to provide complete satisfaction. Women could not only enjoy Dandy Dildo's superior vaginal penetration but if they craved the finest in fellatio it would be possible for them to not only feel they had the real thing in their mouths, but that delicious liquid would ram the backs of their throats and float into their bodies for ultimate joy. My trusty man servant and I donated generous amounts of semen for the project, going far above the norm as we were so devoted to the cause. Now, of course, I had no way of being sure it would work, but, again, my trusted servant came to my rescue, volunteering to suck the enormous member

J. Wayne Frye

and see if it was capable of ejaculation. I was thoroughly surprised that he was so willing to do all he could in service to science. What a man.

Sure enough, it did exactly as I expected and ejaculated with precision. My man servant was so devoted to the cause that he did it again and again just to make certain it was working effectively. Science never had a greater devotee than Harold.

Now, I was ready to give it to my wife for her complete satisfaction when Harold made one other comment that made me decide it was not as perfect as it could be. It had grand length. It had superior circumference. It ejaculated as if it were a cannon. Oh and those hairy balls dangled with dandy delight. I must admit that I was actually motivated to jiggle them myself, but again my man servant Harold volunteered to play with them while he conducted research on how hard it could shoot its load into his mouth. He pronounced Dandy Dildo a resounding success, but I decided there was an element it needed to add to the psychological and emotional aspects of sex. Yes, it needed the ability to speak so that it could moan and groan to compliment the physical aspect of sex. My dear man servant said, "Shall I find a larynx, a warm, fresh voice box to bring it the ability to speak words of endearment when fornication is occurring. I replied in the positive, throwing all morality in regards to murder away with my devotion to science."

CHABLIS AND THE DILDO FROM HELL

I did not ask my dear servant where he got the human parts I needed but they were indeed still warm when he handed them to me. However, there was one important part I had omitted – to form words did the princely prick not need a brain? Long ago I had perfected the ability to miniaturize the brain cells, to separate them out based upon what function they performed. Yes, I could utilize the part of the brain used for speech and implant it in a large knob to be used as a handle to hold the magnificent member with as it was being thrust in and out, in and out. Again Harold arrived within hours with a warm human brain which I operated on and removed the parts I needed. Oh, perfection was now on the laboratory table before me. My man servant gazed along with me in amazement as Dandy Dildo said, "Hey mother-fuckers get me some pussy or ass to fuck."

My dear man servant, with superior devotion to science, dropped his pants and crawled up on Dandy Dildo, riding it gleefully in the name of science. The two of them experienced a mind blowing orgasm with verbalization so loud it cracked the ceiling wall.

The two of them lay there, my man servant moaning. It was already one in the morning; the rain pattered dismally against the panes, and my candle was nearly burnt out as was my man servant, when, by the glimmer of the half-extinguished light, I heard a faint whisper from

CHABLIS AND THE DILDO FROM HELL

Dandy Dildo, "I need more than that asshole. I need me some pussy dude. I need some moist warm pussy. Come on, get me what I desire or I'll fuck the both of you until you haemorrhage from my pounding. Then, a convulsive motion agitated its testicles as they began to wiggle from side to side.

How can I describe my emotions, or how do I delineate the wretch whom with such infinite pains and care I had endeavoured to form? Then I looked over at Harold who was still recovering from the ecstasy of the ramming he had received. He looked at me and his eyes rolled back in his head. He was exhausted.

I had worked hard for so long, for the sole purpose of infusing life into an inanimate object. For this I had deprived myself of rest and health. I had desired it with intense ardour; but now that I had finished, the beauty of the dream vanished, and breathless horror and disgust filled my heart.

Unable to endure the reality of the monstrous thing I had created, I rushed out of the room and continued a long time traversing about the house, unable to compose my mind to sleep. At length lassitude succeeded to the tumult I had before endured, and I threw myself naked on the bed beside my sleeping wife, endeavouring to seek a few moments of forgetfulness by playing with her magnificent derriere.

CHABLIS AND THE DILDO FROM HELL

As I fondled her beautiful, soft skin I could not resist parting her cheeks and playing devilishly with that little brown hole. She began to moan and as was her custom said, "Get that tongue in there bitch. Lick it, kiss it, explore it and worship it." Overcome with lust, I did as she said, but as I was enjoying myself, I suddenly remembered that Harold had been left alone with that abomination. He was too exhausted to fight any advances, and what might happen when Dandy Dildo let lose with his uncontrollable lustful urges.

I suddenly raised my head from between her cheeks and looked to my left. It was Dandy Dildo lying on the bed next to us. I said, as my wife looked back at me first, then at it, "Run dear, run. It is loose."

She started to leap up, but as she turned on her back, the evil thing leaped into the air and with its mighty balls slapped me so hard in the face I was knocked off the bed onto the floor, and though it did not have eyes or limbs, I could feel some mesmerizing force holding me down. Oh, the horror of it all, as Dandy Dildo apparently leapt upon my wife's gapping hole and started furiously pounding in and out. Before long, she was moaning with pleasure shouting, "fuck it baby, fuck it hard." With each thrust the thing let out a guttural sound as if it was some wild beast. Suddenly, my wife exploded in a mind blowing orgasm as Dandy Dildo kept pumping away.

J. Wayne Frye

CHABLIS AND THE DILDO FROM HELL

My wife lay exhausted on the bed and the thing rolled toward me as if it had eyes fixed on me. My wife rolled over to grab it and without hesitation wrapped her slender right hand around its girth and said as she lay face down and started to ease it into her anus, "give it to me here baby, please. Don't deny me your pleasure tool."

I wanted to jump up and crush the thing with all my might, but within it was a mind that now had inordinate power to control and paralyze. I simply could not move as I watched it pound Kandy furiously as she moaned and shouted "harder, harder." Finally, the damnable instrument of pleasure exploded in her, and she let out a scream so loud it cracked the dresser mirror. She again collapsed in exhaustion, sighing with delight as that monstrous dildo rolled out of the room. I went to her but all she could utter was, "get it baby, please. I must have more, please."

Determined to destroy my invention, I went to the laboratory hoping that perhaps it had retuned there, but alas, the shock at what I saw made me realize that I had unleashed a vile evil into the world. Harold lay sprawled on the laboratory gurney face down with his legs spread wide. His poor buttock was torn savagely apart with at least a one foot opening staring me in the face. His anus had been literally ripped apart in a horrible fornicating frenzy. He had given his life for science.

J. Wayne Frye   51

CHABLIS AND THE DILDO FROM HELL

Chablis looked up at the clock on the far wall, and as she tried to control her laughter she looked over at Mr. Broughton who was still in deep sleep. Wiping the smile off her face, she got up and walked around the room for awhile, shaking her head in disbelief. Surely nobody really believed this fantastic tale.

She sat back down, crossed her legs and had to admit that although the story was amusing that it was also titillating her libido as she was thinking about her trusty dildo that had brought her pleasure often, but this dildo sounded like an incredible mind-blowing orgasmic experience. She looked over at Mr. Broughton and found herself wondering what it would be like to fuck an 82 year old man. Surely he couldn't get an erection anymore. Hey, she would need Carlton that night. He had gone into Brattleboro, but would be back around 7 and she definitely had plans for him.

She picked up the book, and began to read again. There were details about how the dildo escaped from the estate, and how Karson had dumped Harold's body in the nearby swamp in order to avoid any embarrassing investigation. After all, were they going to put a dildo in jail for murder? No, the only way out was to destroy the thing that Karson had created, and all the while he was desperately trying to locate the dildo his wife kept asking him when could she play with it again?

J. Wayne Frye

CHABLIS AND THE DILDO FROM HELL

The story continued as follows: *On the road to town a young lawyer named Harvey Grumman was driving his Model-T when he came across something strange just rolling down the road to his left. He stopped his car, got out and went over to the left side of the road near a clump of grass. Looking down he saw Dandy Dildo. He reached down, picked it up and felt its warmness as he examined it thoroughly. He tossed the thing in the back seat, thinking it would be fun to show it to his girlfriend that night and tell her that when he was away it could be her companion. Driving into town, he feared that someone might see it in the car, so he put it in his briefcase and went into the court where he had a case scheduled to go to trial that afternoon at 2.*

An evil incarnation endued with animation could not be as hideous as that wretch of fornicating frenzy in the briefcase. I had gazed upon it with neglect; and did not initially see its ugliness, but watching my wife writhing in misery as she longed for its sexual prowess, her carnal instincts rendering her incapable of any thought but the desire to be possessed by Dandy Dildo, put me in a frenzied search for it. It was as if the life was going out of her each hour, each minute and each second that she could not be enjoying the furious pounding. I knew not where to look but I would later find out what had happened in court that day, and the occurrence would be henceforth called the day of sexual terror.

J. Wayne Frye 53

CHABLIS AND THE DILDO FROM HELL

As Chablis read the following pages, she reflected on how much things had changed in the USA since those days, because the lawyer who had Dandy Dildo in his briefcase, Harvey Grumman, walked into the courthouse without having to pass through metal detectors. The second amendment had, at this time, not been abused by the fanatics who believed a gun spitting lead was the way to solve all society's problems.

She continued reading: *That day in the court, the young lawyer placed his suitcase on the table in the courtroom and suddenly the case popped open, and before the stunned eyes of all there Dandy jumped out shouting "I'll fuck you all." Men and women ran in a frenzied fear, and the bailiff fired off several rounds at what he said was a dancing dildo with big dangling balls. Later it would be said that someone had apparently practiced mass hypnotism that day in the courtroom, but what was the explanation for three women who said that a wild dildo had jumped up their skirts and pounded their pussies with a fury? As they told the story, they were smiling from ear to ear. Finally, the dildo was seen hoping out the front door and down the steps as women ran after him shouting "do me, do me" and another bailiff spit lead from his gun at Dandy Dildo who rolled into a nearby forest and disappeared.*

CHABLIS AND THE DILDO FROM HELL

CHAPTER 4
THE REST OF THE STORY IS A TRAGEDY

That hot member can make it rain on your slit
Baby, Dandy Dildo can cause a sexual fit
Dandy Dildo was invented for passion
It seems to offer great satisfaction

It is a magic stick that throws away pride
That damn thing is messing with your mind
It dives into that paradise hole
And rams up into your soul

Dandy Dildo is always on duty my dear
So lack of satisfaction you never fear
In loneliness you will never cry
This thing will ride you until you die

It cannot lick but wow can it pound
Making you want to keep it around
It makes you feel so good
You'd marry it if you could.

CHABLIS AND THE DILDO FROM HELL

Chablis continued to read, passing the day with a broad smile on her face, and she strangely began to feel her libido rise as she read more. She even found her mind wandering into flights of fantasy about her glorious dildo that often brought her sexual release when no man was around to answer the call to duty. Sometimes her pulse beat so quickly and hardily that she felt the palpitation of every artery; feeling a languor and extreme weakness as the words she was reading, though ridiculous, were having an effect on her as she felt a rise between her legs and the relaxation of her sphincter muscles that always contracted so easily to welcome a dildo or the real thing into the chamber of pleasure.

Looking about the room, she found herself again wondering what it would be like to have sex with an 82 year old man. Aaron Adams, her erstwhile partner, at 62, was the oldest man she had ever had sex with, and though it was wonderful, the two had decided it was only a one time thing that they would treasure forever. However, as she looked over at James Broughton, she noticed that he had a firm outline in the left side of his pants. Damn, he probably had a monster cock, but, no doubt, it had been flaccid for years. Still, as she put down the book, she looked over and gazing upon his obviously monster member slowly eased her right hand up her dress, pushing it back to her little panties as she lifted her pelvis so she could feel her anal opening and gently massage it slowly and

J. Wayne Frye

then more vigorously, all the time staring at the outline of James Broughton's monstrous member. She began to sigh with passion as she slid two fingers into her massive opening.

She eased her head back and stared at the ceiling as she worked her hole feverously. She closed her eyes and drifted into that place where ecstasy dwells deep within and the oblivion of sexual delight floats about like a soft cloud on the horizon of harmonious fulfillment. She felt a hand on the back of her head as it slowly pushed it downward gliding her mouth toward a rock hard monstrous member that was pulsating with desire. She never opened her eyes, only felt her way forward with instinct, swallowing the object in one giant gobbling motion and then with total devotion to the cause sucked it like a high powered vacuum cleaner devouring everything in its sight. Whoever it was began pumping hard and furious.

Chablis eased off on the suction so they could both get maximum enjoyment out of it. He let out a low, slow moan when she put one of his balls into my mouth. She swished it around inside her mouth, and then switched to the other one. She was also stroking his thighs with her hands. He started breathing hard when she managed to put both his balls into her mouth at once. She tenderly licked his balls while warming them up with her hot mouth. She used her tongue to move them all around; her lips were completely enveloping his entire sack, up to the root of his member. She was not sucking it. She was worshipping it.

"Oh, Chablis!" He didn't seem capable of saying much else. She liked that; turning a guy on so much he couldn't really speak. "Oh Chablis," he moaned again in a deep, aged gravelly voice. She loved hearing her own name murmured out in pleasure. Still, she had not opened her eyes as she was enjoying the thrill of sucking without knowing who it was, but she actually did know who it was. Still, they were both enjoying the playful anonymity

She removed his balls from her mouth and licked his shaft with the tip of her tongue. She drenched it with her saliva. Starting at the root, she worked her way up to the sensitive underside right under the head. She gave that area some licks, and then teased him a bit with some long slow licks up and down the shaft. When she knew he really needed some more direct stimulation, she finally put my lips around the whole head and began the furious sucking again. Fondling his balls with her right hand, she slowly lowered her mouth over his entire organ, getting it deep inside and moaning as she devoured every bit of it.

She slowly bobbed her head up and down on his member, getting her hands under him and squeezing his wrinkly butt. She could hear his breathing getting heavier. She knew he was deeply enjoying himself. She stopped for just a second so she could answer a question that always lingered in a man's mind when he was getting a blow job. "Don't worry baby. Let it squirt away. I swallow! Just let your load flow into my mouth."

Chablis loved swallowing because it made her feel so empowered, making a man blow his load inside her throat because she got him off. He began to buck his hips up and down as she stroked the root of his member with her hands and swallowed his shaft again. Swirling her tongue wildly around the underside of the head, she drove him mad with desire. He was sweating profusely. She could feel it on his thighs, brushing against her face. He kept groaning and moaning with pleasure as she became more firm and determined with her sucking. She drooled and slobbered all over his root, trying to make the blowjob as wet and messy as possible.

She eased up a bit and let it pop out of her mouth as she said, "I love being your cock-sucking slut. She immediately gobbled it up again and willingly resumed the furious sucking."

"Oh, Chablis, Oh, it feels so good," he moaned.

She made sexual sounds to excite him; years of willful practice had taught her that men love hearing erotic moans from women, even if they are just for effect.

CHABLIS AND THE DILDO FROM HELL

"Mmm..."she murmured! She swished his hot rod inside her cheeks, getting it as deep into her throat as possible while breathing through her nose. She was buried into his lap; his member completely inside her mouth, his thighs pressed up against her cheeks. Her eyelashes brushed up against his pubic hair.

"Oh Chablis, I'm cumming. I can't hold it much longer."

She didn't answer him verbally. She just sucked him faster and made moaning noises as she prepared to finish him off. Her pace and intensity grew with each trip up and down his organ. She made loud slurping and sucking sounds with her mouth. His member was rock hard and throbbing. She could feel it shaking. She visualized the hot white joy juice loaded up in his balls getting ready to squirt hard.

"Oh my! Oh my!" The contractions began, and his erection flexed. She focused the muscles of her mouth and tongue intently on the head while tightening her grip around his balls. She felt the pre-cum that she had tasted all throughout the blowjob start to drip out even more. Then the explosion came with hurricane force, slamming into the back of her throat with a fury. She bobbed her head up and down and forced herself to quickly swallow it up, not wanting to lose a drop. He grabbed her boobs tightly as the intensity of the orgasm made him need something to hold on to.

Spurt after spurt of hot joy juice shot down her throat. She gulped it down enthusiastically. Just when she thought it was over, his throbbing rod quivered with some involuntary aftershocks, and yet more creamy juice trickled down her throat. She kept his rock hard erection in her mouth after the main part of the orgasm ended, and there was drop after drop of cum still dripping out of the head even though the huge spurting phase had ended. Still, she had not opened her eyes, as the idea of a mind-blowing anonymous suck was titillating her to the point that her normally useless member squirted its joy juice spontaneously. She let out a long, slow moan and felt his cock slowly go soft as he pulled it out of her mouth.

Still, with eyes closed, she heard him walk out of the room. Slowly she opened her eyes and looked over at the now vacant chair where James had been sitting. She reached over and picked up the book and started to read again knowing nothing Dandy Dildo did could top what she just did, but alas, she would be surprised.

———

Mingled with horror, I searched the village and neighbouring towns for Dandy Dildo. I felt the bitterness of disappointment; dreams that had

CHABLIS AND THE DILDO FROM HELL

been my food and pleasant rest for so long a space had now become a hell to me; and the change was so rapid, the overthrow so complete. What had I wrought upon mankind with the invention that was now destroying my mind and wrecking havoc across the village and town where men were becoming obsolete as none could match the sexual prowess of Dandy Dildo?

Morning, dismal and wet, at length dawned and came to my sleepless and aching eyes the church of the village, its white steeple and clock soaring high in the misty morning air. I longed for my forlorn wife who writhed in agonies of desire for Dandy Dildo. I felt impelled to hurry on, although wetted by the morning dew which flittered down from a black and comfortless sky. I continued walking to where I did not know. I just meandered in an aimless manner for some time, endeavouring by bodily exercise to ease the load that weighed upon my mind. I traversed the streets without any clear conception of where I was or what I was doing. My heart palpitated in the sickness of fear, and I hurried on with irregular steps, realizing the evil that I had unleashed on mankind.

It was when I turned the corner of Main Street and Appleton Avenue in Brattleboro that I remembered a poem I had once read:

Like one who, on a lonely road,
Doth walk in fear and dread,

CHABLIS AND THE DILDO FROM HELL

And, having once turned round, walks on,
And turns no more his head;
Because he knows a frightful fiend
Doth close behind him tread.

I trembled excessively; I could not endure to think of, and far less to allude to, the occurrences of the preceding weeks that had led to me producing not hope for mankind, but now maybe the end of mankind as women would no longer be willing to procreate but rather only seek out Dandy Dildo. I kept looking behind me, feeling that I was somehow being stalked. I was now in fear that it knew what I was going to do and that somehow it was going to eliminate me first. I dreaded to behold this monster, but I had to eliminate it. I carried despondency still and went back home where I was greeted by a servant with horrible news. My dear wife was upstairs inconsolable with grief and no one could lift her spirits. I knew what she longed for, what she was obsessed with that was gnawing away at her soul. She was longing for Dandy Dildo.

Chablis had enjoyed a dildo often, but reflecting back upon what had recently occurred, she realized that nothing could ever replace the real thing. She licked her lips and thought what a thrill sucking an 82 year old man. Damn, it was fun, and he had really enjoyed it. That was what brought her so much joy, being able to control men with her mouth. "Damn," she thought. "I'm good."

CHABLIS AND THE DILDO FROM HELL

As she was about to pick up the book, in walked Carlton and he had a spring in his step as he said, "Just passed my dad in the hallway. Never seen such a smile on his face, you didn't blow him did you?"

Not being one to kiss and tell, she replied, "Of course not, but he is a good looking older man. You better watch your step."

Looking down at the book, he said, "So, are you up to snuff on the history of Dandy Dildo?"

"I am up to the part where he is now searching for his invention to destroy it, and he has discovered his wife is enraptured in the web of eroticism spun by Dandy Dildo."

"Well, there is much more, but to sum it up, Karson's wife eventually committed suicide as her husband could not locate Dandy Dildo. She longed for it so frightfully that she eventually killed herself when he refused to create a duplicate in his laboratory."

"And you can provide absolute proof of all this?"

"Well, let's be honest. It has been almost 100 years since the incident. Anyone connected to this is long dead, but there might be some relatives still around."

CHABLIS AND THE DILDO FROM HELL

The night was spent fornicating for hours with Carlton, and the next morning, as she and James Broughton sat at the dining room table, they kept glancing at each other and she knew that the old man was looking forward to another session with her. She thought that she had probably unleashed a caged tiger now, as he was feeling renewed virility and wanting to prove his manhood. Men were such ninnies she thought, but she felt herself strangely more attracted to the old man than the son. She got up and left with a dire warning for the two men. "I am going to investigate, but frankly, I think it will be an exercise in futility, because I think the whole thing is a fantastic fairy tale. Still, I can appreciate that finding the item would indeed be interesting. Maybe some museum would pay handsomely for it."

Her journey was filled with recollections of the time she spent with the two men, but she kept concentrating on her encounter with James. She wished to hurry on, for she longed to get to the bottom of the case as quickly as possible. She could hardly sustain the multitude of feelings that crowded into her mind. An uneasy feeling overcame her. She wandered to the ruins of the Karson estate. The road ran by the side of the lake there, which became narrower as she approached the Karson home. There were grass hills around the estate, the sky and lake were both azure blue and placid. There was a disquieting stillness to the place, an intense loneliness.

CHABLIS AND THE DILDO FROM HELL

As she drew nearer the home, trepidation overcame her. Night also closed around. The place appeared a vast and dim scene of evil. As she walked about the estate, the sky was serene; and, she wondered about the laboratory and the place where Harold was murdered by an overactive sexually demanding Dandy Dildo. A terrible storm began to brew and she sought shelter inside the ruins. The most violent part of the storm hung exactly north of her. She looked around and realized she was in the former laboratory and there was the gurney where Harold had been brutally sexually assaulted by Dandy Dildo and literally torn apart by the furious ramming he received.

While she watched the tempest, so beautiful yet darkly foreboding, she wandered on with a hasty step. This noble war in the sky elevated to a continuous rumbling of thunder. She noticed a short figure out of the side of her eyes. It was basically nothing more than a shadow, but still she reached down, lifted her skirt and removed her snub-nosed 38 from its thigh holster. She cradled it in her right hand and stood silently. The tiny figure was visible through the open archway as the door had been removed. She stood fixed, gazing intently. A flash of lightning illuminated the object, and the shape was obvious. Her heart raced as she looked down at the shadow in the distance. It was no more than 12, maybe 14 inches high. It was the shape of a dildo. What was it doing there? Could it be Dandy Dildo? She laughed.

CHABLIS AND THE DILDO FROM HELL

She was imagining things. Still, she was not prone to flight of fantasy. The figure passed down the hallway and she heard a muffled giggle.

She thought of pursuing the thing, but it would have been in vain, for she was unfamiliar with her surroundings, and whatever that thing was it knew the home intimately. The giggling trailed off and she knew it had scurried out of the home, whatever it was. She remained motionless for a couple of seconds. The thunder ceased, but the rain still continued, and the scene was enveloped in an impenetrable darkness. Though a bit disconcerting, she was not overly concerned. She waited until the rain stopped, went home and enjoyed an evening of fornicating with Carlton, although at dinner, she found herself constantly looking at James and wanting to suck him again. There was something special about the elderly gentlemen that simply titillated her. She called Aaron first thing in the morning and gave him the details on how the investigation was going. He suggested she try to find someone who might give some sort of details on what happened almost 100 years ago, surely, he said, there must be some grandchildren or maybe even some children around who could remember their mothers and Dandy Dildo.

Day dawned and she directed her efforts towards the town. She still assumed the story was nothing more than an elaborate fairy tale formed by some pranksters to put a bit of excitement in their lives. Yes, Karson was nothing but a fun-loving prankster who had developed an incredible hoax that was endued with a life all its own that was picked up by person after person and embellished more and more.

She went to the town librarian for information on the Karson family and the mysterious tales about them. The librarian, a Ms. Diane Foster, who was well into her 70's, and with a smile of attribution, pointed Chablis toward the rare book room. She ushered her in, closed and locked the door behind them and pointed to a desk, indicating she should take a seat. Thus began an interesting discourse. "Ms. Chavez, you are looking at a librarian who has led a life of debauchery."

Chablis, looking intently at the 5 feet tall, maybe 50 kilos (110 pounds) tops, demure, dainty woman said, "Really?"

"Oh yes, my mother taught me as a teenager to enjoy my sexuality as her mother had taught her. You see, my grandmother, was the third or fourth person to experience the euphoric fornicating of an instrument known as Dandy Dildo."

Chablis had not mentioned the dildo specifically, but she nodded her head affirmatively as she said, "So, please tell me all you know about this thing called Dandy Dildo."

CHABLIS AND THE DILDO FROM HELL

"Ever since I accidentally brushed my anus with the showerhead when I was 14, I got to thinking how good it felt and wondered what it would be like to try out some masturbation with something in there. Ms. Chavez I popped my anal cherry with a rock hard cucumber."

"I finally decided why not give it a try so initially I ordered a realistic 9 inch dildo in a catalogue and made sure I got the mail every day so my mom would not intercept the package. The thought of it being forbidden was titillating for me, but I was sure my mom would have probably confiscated it and used it on herself. Little did I know what I was going to discover upon arrival."

Chablis was simply overcome with the candor of this old woman who had no shame whatsoever about her sexuality. She continued her story. "It was late at night and I was by myself. I was furiously masturbating myself with my index and forefinger. The dildo had arrived in a plain wrapper – and it was by my bed. I was just a little girl. But I had been thinking about it on and off all day and it had been driving me crazy with anticipation. Running the thought of the dildo in my anus around in my mind while I stroked myself furiously, I began to moan with delight as I grabbed the dildo and the lube. I was ready to pop it into my gaping ass. I covered the head of the dildo with lube, and let it run down all round, making sure it was properly covered. Then I held it firmly by the base, and lifted my legs into the air while placing the head of the dildo against my anus. My heart was pounding. My hands were shaking in anticipation, which actually made it feel fantastic as it was like a vibrator!"

Chablis, not one to ever be put off by sex, but pressed for time, interrupted her, "Ma'am, I frankly don't see what your personal experience has to do with what happened nearly 100 years ago with something called Dandy Dildo. What is your point?"

"Please be patient and you will understand my point. You see, I am 86 years old, and this happened when I was 14 years old."

Nodding her head up and down, Chablis said, "Go ahead, then."

"I had not even put it in my ass yet and it was making me so stimulated I couldn't stand it. I applied some gentle pressure and waited. I turned the dildo from side to side and slowly it went a little ways into my hole. It was amazing. But it stopped and wouldn't go further. I gently continued to push it in and out – a little at the time - only the head of the fake cock would go in. But the sensations were mind blowing. I continued doing this for about five minutes - heart still pounding furiously. I suddenly looked up and there was my mother who had walked in."

CHABLIS AND THE DILDO FROM HELL

"She smiled, turned and started to walk out as she looked over her shoulder and said, 'Finish what you are doing. It is absolutely normal to be curious about sex. When you finish, I will tell you an unbelievable story.' I thought I should maybe stop, but I was so wound up with passion, the fact my mother had seen me did not bother me at all. So I applied pressure where it seemed to stop going in. I was moaning a little at this point, not because it hurt but because I wanted it so badly. I wanted to be so full. Finally my sphincter relented and the dildo slipped in deeper and deeper. My ass was so gloriously full. I started sliding it in and out - my anal cherry was well-rammed and truly popped. It was amazing. After five or six minutes, my eyes rolled back in my head, and I had a mind-blowing orgasm. I had never experienced such a fantastic orgasm in my young life like that before, either while masturbating or with regular sex from a cock. I couldn't take it any more."

"I was ashamed of myself for being such a wanton young girl. That is the point of my story. I need for you to understand that the story of Dandy Dildo first was broached that day because of what I did. I avoided my mother the rest of the evening, but that night, she came to my room and said that I should not be ashamed of what I did as curiosity about sex was healthy. Although we lived then and still do today in a country filled with backwards religious cretins, she was not one."

CHABLIS AND THE DILDO FROM HELL

"It was then that she placed her hand on my left arm as I lay in bed, squeezed it tightly and said that it was time I knew of Dandy Dildo."

Chablis breathed a sigh of relief. Finally, she thought, after all that she can get to what I need to hear. However, she giggled a bit inside as she realized how much fun the old lady was having sharing the sex story.

"Now, what I am about to tell you will seem fantastic, but I believe it, because I never knew my mother to lie."

"OK, I believe you, but please get to the point."

"I call the story *My Grandmother and the Dandy Dildo*. So, this is the whole story as it was told to me. It is about her and her mother. Like us, my mom and her mother had an open relationship where no subject was taboo. They told each other everything. So one day, a very, very sad day, after my mom had left home to live with a boyfriend at 18, her mom's house burned down. My grandmother was at work, but she did lose some very dear pets. The firefighters were shoveling things out of the windows to keep the fire from consuming everything - it was a very old house, and went up like kindling. In no time, there was little left but a pile of her smouldering belongings on the front lawn. My mom's husband (who was then her boyfriend) was there, helping her try to pick up what few things they could salvage when all of the sudden, grandmother swooped down, grabbed something, and jammed it into her giant oversized purse.

My mom asked my grandmother what it was and she opened her purse slightly and there it was, an incredibly big and thick dildo, but it seemed to have life to it. Yes, it seemed to actually be breathing, but it was very laboured breathing. And she had the saddest look on her face when she said, 'It may not work anymore.' She bowed her head and had tears in her eyes."

"Now, my grandmother had lost her husband months before, when he just up and disappeared. So, the natural reaction of my mother was that it was just a replacement for the sex she had enjoyed with my grandfather, but it was actually much more than that. My grandmother began to cry and said that she loved the dildo and that it had a name. My mom was shocked but could not resist asking its name. My grandmother replied that its name was Dandy Dildo."

After all this, finally thought Chablis, I am getting to the crux of what this old lady is trying to tell me. She looked at her directly in the eyes and said, "So, this was the dildo that was invented by Karson?"

"It was, yes."

CHABLIS AND THE DILDO FROM HELL

"Please go on. Tell me the rest of the story."

She lowered her head, and tears began to form in her eyes as she looked up at Chablis. "Oh, the rest of the story is a tragedy."

CHAPTER 5
EUPHORIA OF MIND, BODY AND SPIRIT

Why do I need a man?
To help me open doors?
Excuse me if I'm wrong,
But what are my hands for?

Why do I need a man?
To help me do hard work?
I am just as capable,
Even though I wear a skirt

Why do I need a man?
To pick me up when I'm down?
I stand on my own two feet
When no one else is around

Why do I need a man?
So I can have a family some day?
I don't want to look fat and ugly.
No I'd rather adopt and be gay.

J. Wayne Frye   75

CHABLIS AND THE DILDO FROM HELL

Why do I need a man?
To get some time between the sheets?
A dildo can do the same thing
And batteries are cheap.

Chablis listened intently as the little old lady continued her story. "Chewing on the inside of her cheek to stop herself from laughing at her mom, she fought back the urge to tease her, because my grandmother was so earnest as she kept opening the huge handbag to check on the dildo's state."

"My mom told her not to worry as she would get her a new one, but my poor grandmother was in tears as she professed to be in love with Dandy Dildo."

"My mom told her that they could take it to its inventor, Mr. Karson and maybe he could repair it, so that it vibrated properly and worked as well as it once did. However, my grandmother nearly went berserk, insisting that the dildo would be destroyed by its inventor. She wrapped both her arms around the purse, pulled it tightly to her chest and insisted that she would never do that for the dildo was deathly afraid of its inventor. Needless to say, my mom thought that my grandmother had simply gone off the deep end, but she elected to humour her because of what had happened. Obviously, she was having an incredibly traumatic reaction to the horrible fire which had destroyed her home."

CHABLIS AND THE DILDO FROM HELL

Chablis, by this time, was enthralled with the story, and waited enthusiastically for the next chapter in the saga. The little old lady continued her story. "So, my grandmother lived at my mother's apartment, sleeping on the sofa. All throughout her time there she actually would sleep with Dandy Dildo by her side, wrapping her arms around it as if it were a human being. She stroked it, kissed it and talked to it. My mom was beginning to think a psychiatrist was the only answer. However, after about a week, she walked into the living room one morning and my grandmother was being furiously banged by the dildo that had apparently recovered from whatever malady it had suffered. My mother was in shock as she watched my grandmother lying there and the dildo appeared to be alive, alive with fornicating devilishness that was making my grandmother wiggle and squirm with delight. She just looked up at my mother, unashamed and said, 'it made me kill your father, but I am not ashamed. I love it. I love it. It is all I live for.' So, shocked, but not totally convinced that the dildo had somehow exercised control over my grandmother, my mother went back into her bedroom and debated on whether to call the police or not. After all, my grandmother had just admitted to murdering my grandfather for the love of a dildo. Surely, if she had indeed killed him she could easily get off on an insanity plea, because my mother was now convinced that she was stark-raving crazy, totally bonkers."

CHABLIS AND THE DILDO FROM HELL

"My mom had to go to work. She assumed my grandmother would go to work, too. However, something horrible happened while she was away. When she came home at the end of the day, my grandmother was lying on the sofa, her legs spread wide and her vagina was as wide as a whale's grin. The doctor's autopsy said she died of heart failure apparently from experiencing too many orgasms. Dandy Dildo was gone, and my mother was too embarrassed to mention my mother's fascination with that damned abomination and her admission to the murder of my grandfather whose body has never been found."

Chablis thought that maybe she should look upon all the ravings of these people about Dandy Dildo as some type of mass insanity. What would people think of her if she told them she was searching for a nearly 100 year old dildo that had been complacent in murder? She thanked the old woman and walked out of the library and wondered what would be her next step in what was becoming the strangest case she had ever tackled.

How could she locate a fugitive dildo? She laughed at the question as she walked down the main street of Brattleboro, taking in the quaint beauty of the place. Nearly 100 years had elapsed since Karson's invention. She meandered toward the Brattleboro Bugle Newspaper office and asked to go through its morgue.

J. Wayne Frye

CHABLIS AND THE DILDO FROM HELL

She was ushered into a cubicle, where she sat behind an old microfiche machine and was handed boxes of files from the early 1900's. She poured over them meticulously, looking for anything that might hint of a connection with Dandy Dildo.

Nothing is more painful to the human mind than, after the feelings have been worked up by a quick succession of events, the dead calmness of inaction and certainties which follow that deprives the soul of hope. The old lady's grandmother had died a horrible death by orgasm. O.K., maybe as deaths go that is not so bad thought Chablis, but dead is still dead, and just how much truth was there to the story.

She reflected on what had transpired all those years ago and the deeds of mischief were beyond description. Karson had begun his quest with benevolent intentions and thirsted for the moment when he should put them in practice and make his invention useful to the sexually frustrated women of the world, and maybe even the gay men who also longed for a good butt ramming. All that was blasted away, as instead of creating sexual serenity he had bestowed the world with an intense, hellacious, torturous manifestation of evil that had reared its ugly head. Chablis' abhorrence of this fiend seemed to be growing. When she thought of Karson, her passions became inflamed, and she ardently wished to extinguish the evil if it did indeed exist or was it all just fanciful fairy tales?

CHABLIS AND THE DILDO FROM HELL

The day wore on as she looked at paper after paper from that era in search of any tiny lead that might help her in the quest to find this evil dildo. Suddenly, she came upon an item in the classified section under the heading Words for Loved Ones: *Darling, I miss you so much. I am so stressed without your physical love, and I hate that you have to worry about that evil man who wants to destroy you. I cannot sit around and do nothing to protect the one who brings me so much physical pleasure. I am dedicated to serving you. It pains me to see you so tired and also so stressed, but believe me; I love you so much that I only want the very best for you in life. I want to make your lot in life better and more progressive, so that you can soar to grand heights of sexual achievement satisfying my desire to worship at your altar of pleasure. Never doubt my complete and total devotion to you, because it is unstinting, unwavering and as solid as the Rock of Gibraltar. In me, you have a champion who like the Knights of old shall always stand by your side with lance in hand on a trusty stead ready to ride to your rescue and serve your cause with undying devotion! I may be a female, but I am still your Knight in shining armour. All my love DD from SJ.*

Chablis went to the clerk and asked if she would have records of all the classifieds placed over the years. She replied affirmatively and handed her the receipt microfiche and said, "Good luck."

CHABLIS AND THE DILDO FROM HELL

Finding the exact date and the exact ad, including price charged and who placed the ad was easy once she found the exact date of the publication. There it was, April 23, 1925, an ad to be placed under *Words for Loved Ones* – ad placed by Sarah Jane McClusky for $1.77. First, why would she place such an ad, and number two, who was she?"

Again Chablis brought out the other microfiche files and started looking for any articles dealing with a person names Sarah Jane McClusky. There were numerous articles in the Society Section where a person named Sarah Jane McClusky prominently appeared as one of the town's more well-known citizen's who was married to Robert McClusky, President of the Brattleboro National Bank. As she continued looking, she came across the front page from May 27th 1925 and it was like a slap in the face when she read the headline: *Prominent Socialite, Sarah Jane McClusky, Charged with Murder of Husband.*

For no apparent reason, she had brutally smothered him in his sleep and cut off his penis, put it on her writing table and wrote some words that were un-publishable. Chablis grabbed her purse, thanked the lady and headed to the police station, where she was greeted like a celebrity as everyone knew of her exploits in New York City. It was easy to get access to the old files as she was escorted to the file storage building and the officer pulled down the box containing all evidence from the case and handed it to her and pointed to a desk in the far corner. She sat down, and with the attendant looking over her shoulders, she shuffled through the files and found the pickled severed penis. She picked it up, as the male attendant smiled. She fondled it longingly, and she could sense him getting excited. Hey, it had been about eight hours since had a taste of Carlton's manhood and she was always horny anyway. She placed the pickled penis down and turned around. She was eye-level with the officer's zipper. His hard-on was obvious, so she looked up and smiled. He was nervous as hell as he looked around to make sure no one could see them, but she had been there and done that before, so she was not nervous at all. She reached up, unzipped his pants and masterfully popped the root of his passion out of his underwear.

She opened a gap in the flap. She went in there.
She sought for a slit in the boxers that had charge
of the basket she asked for,
came to warm flesh, then to hair.
She went on. She found what she hoped for.
She groped. It was large.

He responded to her fondling
in a charming, disarming way:
he unbuckled his belt while she felt.
His pants fell away.
Carefully drawing it out,

CHABLIS AND THE DILDO FROM HELL

she beheld what she held.

The circumcised head was of a master-craft,
with perfectly beveled rim of unusual weight
and the friendliest head. Even relaxed, the shaft
was of noble dimensions
with the wrinkles that indicate
singular powers of extension.

For a second or two,
it lay inert, then suddenly stirred in her hand,
then paused as if frightened
or doubtful of what to do,
and then with a violent jerk began to expand.
By soundless bounds it extended.

It then distended, and by quick
great leaps it rose, it flushed,
it rushed to its full size.
Nearly nine inches long and four inches thick,
a royal column, ineffably solemn and wise.
She tested its length and strength.

She gave it a manual squeeze.
She bunched her fingers
and twirled them about the knob.
She stroked it from top to bottom.
She lowered her head.
She opened her mouth for the job.

The gorgeous organ stood stiffly and straightly out
with a slight flare upwards.

J. Wayne Frye 83

CHABLIS AND THE DILDO FROM HELL

At each beat of his heart it threw
an odd little nod her way.
From the slot of the spout
exuded a drop of transparent viscous goo.

The lair of hair was fair,
Chablis just stared.
The firm vase of his sperm, like a bulging pear,
cradling its handsome Herculean eggs,
swung he as he shoved towards her,
completely shameless now and bare.

She rocked back and forth her mouth on his cock.
She inserted his divine rod
between her lips and closed as tight as she could.
The upright warmth of his member felt so good.
Mad to be had, to be felt and smelled.
Her lips explored the adorable masculinity.

She snuggled, sniffed and moaned.
She lapped up the taste
of its hot hollow.
Her fingers began to drift
on a trek of inspection.
She was on a leisurely tour of wantonness.

Downward in narrowing circles
she playfully strayed.
Encroached on his privates like a poacher,
approached she his prick with gusto,
as she teasingly swerved,
retreated from meeting, only to begin again.

J. Wayne Frye

CHABLIS AND THE DILDO FROM HELL

It pleaded by a pretty imploring kick.
She shifted in divine assent.
She kissed and sucked as she went
it was quick to her licking and slurping.
He pressed his crotch to her chin.
His thighs squirmed with her tongue.

She worked about the head.
His sensations yearned for consummation.
Enlarged, charged, aching to get sucked,
all his pores were open to joy.
She eased off and inspected his erection.
She surveyed it with a stare.

From scrotum level, sighting along the underside
she looked at the forest of pubic hair.
She admired the texture,
the delicate wrinkles and the neat
sutures of the capacious bag.
She adored the grace of male genitalia.

She raised the delicious meat
to her mouth, brought its hard-on to her face.
Slipping her lips round the Byzantine dome
of the massive head, with the tip of her tongue
she caressed the sensitive groove.
He thrilled to the chill.

"That's lovely!" he hoarsely said.
"Go on! Go on!" He pleaded.
Gently, intently, she slid to the massive base
of his tower of power,

J. Wayne Frye   85

CHABLIS AND THE DILDO FROM HELL

paused there a moment down
in the warm moist thicket.

Then she began to retrace
the smooth way to the throbbing crown.
Intrepid excitements swelled at delights to come,
as she descended and ascended
those thick distended walls
back and forth, back and forth.

She grasped his root
between left forefinger and thumb,
and with her right hand tickled
his heavy voluminous balls.
She plunged with a rhythmical lunge
steady, determined and slow.

And at every stroke made she a corkscrew roll
with her warm, pleading tongue.
His soul reeled in the feeling.
He whimpered "Oh,"
as she tongued and squeezed
and rolled and tickled and swung.

Then she pressed on the spot
where the groin is joined to the cock.
The secret sluices of his juices began to unlock.
He melted into what he felt. "Oh Jesus!" he cried.
Waves of immeasurable pleasures mounted his
member in quick spasms.

She lay still in the notch of his crotch

J. Wayne Frye

CHABLIS AND THE DILDO FROM HELL

inhaling his sweat nectar
as he convulsed into her the rich and thick,
the hot spunk that spouted in gouts,
spurted in jet after jet into her willing mouth.

She moaned as she felt the spunk slide.
Oh, she felt so much power from his tower.
She had done it again and was so proud.
Being a man's passion flower
was exhilaratingly liberating for Chablis.
Now, she was filled with spunk and glee!

The two of them let out a satisfied sigh. She looked up at him and winked. He reached down, zipped up and took a deep breath. No words were spoken. She turned and started going through the evidence box again as he placed his hand on her shoulder. She knew he would remember that blow job on his death bed. He would never have another one that measured up. That gave her great pride, knowing she would always be remembered by the men she had blown as the best cock-sucker they ever had. That was almost as good as being remembered as the best detective. For some reason, she reflected on her dear beautiful Filipino friend, Lynton Viñas, the world-famous demon fighter. She thought maybe she would be a big help in the case, as this dildo seemed like a demon more than a sex toy. She could not help but laugh about Lynton, who was opened minded about sex too, but was not as blatantly promiscuous as Chablis was. Chablis thought to herself, "I am an unmitigated whore and proud of it."

She rifled through the box and glanced over her shoulder at the officer. "Reflection on crimes like this motivates my hatred and the desire for revenge that bursts all bounds of moderation."

He squeezed her shoulder slightly and said, "It was a terrible crime. People rarely speak of it, but you do know what happened to her?"

"No, please tell me."

"Well, I only speak of what I have been told. She was declared insane. She insisted that a dildo had literally come to life and captured her body and soul, telling her to kill her husband. The jury was for death, but the judges in those days had discretion before the right-wing religious hypocrites hijacked the country and insisted on maximum retribution and no rehabilitation. He intervened and declared her mentally incompetent to stand trial based upon the testimony of three psychiatrists who declared her absolutely bonkers. A few weeks later, she was found in the asylum bathroom propped up between two brooms, one inserted in her vagina and the other in her butt. She left a note saying, *I want to go out like a pig skewered over a barbeque pit, dying with an intense, mind-blowing orgasm, one like I received when fucking my dear, sweet, lovable Dandy Dildo.*"

CHABLIS AND THE DILDO FROM HELL

"So, she saw no beauty in the earth without her dildo? Her only accents of love were ineffectual. Sometimes people can cope with the sullen despair that overwhelms them, but sometimes the whirlwind passions of the soul drive people to intolerable solutions. Were there any other cases at all similar to hers? You work here in the files department; surely you have been curious about this case. Come on now, share what you know."

"Well, there is not much to share Chablis. You see, it has been nearly 100 years and what happened was long before the media frenzies where they send down those gorgeous blond bimbos who think the are news people to exploit and titillate the public who are too dumb to know they are being brainwashed and manipulated with tripe. However, there was one young boy in early 1926 who was, I believe only 5 at the time. His mother was arrested for the murder of his father. She blamed what was assumed to be a non-existent dildo that she said played with her mind, urging her to kill. The decision was made not to pursue a trial as it was obvious that she was insane. The boy had secretly watched while his mother had been playing with the dildo, but was too young and naïve to really understand what was happening. He did say to the judge: 'it was in my mom, in my mom, in my mom.' He was interviewed by psychiatrists, but nothing came of it. The boy is alive. He lives at 445 Morton Avenue."

CHABLIS AND THE DILDO FROM HELL

Chablis arose, kissed him on the cheek and whispered. Yummy yum yum – thank you so much for the information and the protein."

She was shocked with his eloquence when he said, "Beauty is a commodity that transcends time, place and distance. It lies on the shores of hope and rests in the grains of lust upon a sunlit day that shines the bright beacon of affection. Your beauty is beyond description, because it goes far beyond the physical. You have given me a day I shall treasure until my last breath."

She said nothing; just smiled and walked out, knowing that he was just one of many who felt that way. Hey, it was only a blow job, but each time she did it to a man it was mystical, doing more than relieving sexual tension – it relieved their souls of untold burdens and made them soar into a euphoria of mind, body and spirit.

J. Wayne Frye

CHAPTER 7
ANGELIC ACT OF KINDNESS

Acts of kindness are about you,
Not just the person receiving benevolence.
Making someone feel good brings pleasure
To the giver as well as the receiver.

The immense mountains towered nearby, and the sun reflected off the buildings dancing delightfully about the sidewalk as Chablis made her way toward the home of Leland Martin, who was 94 years old, and probably well-off, as in the USA, only the rich lived to be old, as the poor could not afford quality healthcare. Welcome to profit based medicine, where service is rendered to those who can afford it thought Chablis as she turned into 445 Morton and made her way up to the front porch that was neat, tidy and reminded her of those old black and white movies with Craftsman style homes lining the streets of middle America at a time when all was delightfully right with the country. Well, except when you were in Brattleboro and Dandy Dildo was on the lose, that is. She giggled at the thought that she was actually beginning to believe just a bit of the strange tale as she rang the door bell.

To her surprise, a very well-dressed thin debonair white haired old man of perhaps 6:2 in height opened the door and smiled broadly at her. He tilted his head to the right and said, "Well, well, my goodness, it is not often a man my age gets a visit some such a beautiful woman. I usually ask for young nurses when I am afforded the privilege of a home visit, but none of them look like you. I don't recall calling for a visit."

"Oh, I am not a nurse. I am Chablis Louise Chavez, a private investigator."

"Wow. I know you. I've seen you in the news a time or two. From New York City, right?"

Nodding affirmatively, Chablis said. "I'd like to ask you a few questions if I may Mr. Martin."

"Dear girl, you can ask me anything you want. Come on in," he said as he stepped to one side so Chablis could enter. He pointed toward the old fashioned parlour on his right and they went in.

Not all homes are created equal. Most are built using cookie-cutter designs and builder-grade materials. This one had been that way at one time, but over the years it had obviously been upgraded. There were those features of sophisticated architectural details and custom flourishes that made you realize that you were in a place that was not a house. It was a home. The soft, relaxing ambiance made Chablis not sit, but rather easily glide into the Queen Ann chair in front of the fireplace. She took a deep breath and looked around in awe of a place that made her feel like she had returned to the turn of the 20th century. The tasteful elegance was almost overpowering.

Mr. Martin said, "Lovely and peaceful isn't it? I was born here you know. I have lived here my whole life. It was my wife who decorated the place, remodelled it to perfection. We were married for 65 years. She has been gone six years now. But hey, today is a grand and glorious day. Like her," he said as he pointed to her picture on the fireplace mantel, "you are a lady of exceptional beauty."

"Well thank you," said Chablis as she looked at a picture of a very young woman on the mantel, "and to compare me to that lovely woman is indeed a compliment. She is, no doubt, your lovely wife. Beauty is a commodity that transcends time, place and distance. It lies on the shores of hope and rests in the grains of love upon a sunlit day that shines the bright beacon of affection."

Continuing his delightfully mischievous smile, he said, "I'll bet you have men chasing after you all the time."

"Well, I do alright, I suppose."

Brushing back his white hair with his right hand, he became more direct. "And what can an old man do for such a beautiful young woman. I know what I wish I could do, but I am afraid those days are long gone."

Giggling, Chablis replied. "I am afraid I have something rather indelicate to ask."

Without hesitation, he said, "My mother's little escapade with impropriety. You are investigating a case and somehow my mother's name popped up."

"I am afraid yes, Mr. Martin. I know you were just a little boy and it was long ago, but any recollections you could share would be invaluable to me."

"Long ago yes. Recollections? They are even clearer now than they were way back then. My mother and father were immensely happy before that infernal thing was brought into the house. I do not want to appear overly crude, but if you want a detailed description of things, it cannot be avoided."

CHABLIS AND THE DILDO FROM HELL

"Believe me; in my business delicate ears would be a handicap. Say what you must in order to provide me with details that might assist me."

"Well, I shall provide all the details I can, but I warn you that you are dealing with evil."

"I have dealt with evil often Mr. Martin. Unfortunately it is not a rare commodity in a world where the difference between good and evil is far too blurred. Those who define themselves as good are often only masquerading in the cloak of righteousness."

"Sounds like fundamentalist Christians to me. I am as sick of them as I am the Muslims. Don't really see any difference except the Christians don't chop off heads, but rather chop off compassion. Damn hypocrites make me sick."

"Well, we are in agreement there."

Wiping his brow with his left hand, he said, "Ah, but it is the incident with my mother that concerns you. Well, it was a sordid affair I suppose. You see, I had no idea what a dildo was, but my mother came in one day carrying a medium size box, looked at me, told me to sit down on the sofa and not bother her for awhile. She went into her bedroom, and I did as asked for almost two hours as I listened to intense moaning coming from the bedroom. This went on for weeks, until one day my curiosity got the best of me. I slipped outside and went to her bedroom window. The curtains were only partially drawn and I watched with fascination as she would plunge that infernal thing in and out of her in a wild frenzy of copulating contagion of excitement that made her seem possessed."

At that point, Chablis interjected, "Obviously, I know what a dildo looks like but could you describe this one in detail?"

"All these years have only solidified my observational reaction. I am a man who has always enjoyed sex, and understood its power over all humanity, but I tell you this instrument was evil. You could see and feel it. Yes, it was a pleasure machine, but it used that pleasure for evil purposes not for the good it should have been used for. It looked pretty realistic with veins and was a bit dark in colour, dark brown it was. Oh, its length and girth were gargantuan, but my mother could not get enough off it. You see, she did not even have her hands upon it. It had a life all its own as it pumped in and out of her hole. With her hands she stroked her body and the look upon her face was one of ecstasy as I have never seen in any women since then. Now, each day I would slip around and watch, and soon she was taking it out of her vagina, and putting it in her butt which seemed to bring her even more delirious pleasure. Again, she did not even touch the thing. It seemed to ram her completely on its own. She would buck up to meet each stroke, and she would often take it out for awhile, lie beside it with the head next to her ear as if it was whispering something to her. After awhile, she would then put it in her mouth and suck furiously, and again it would begin to pump hard and then the damn thing would ejaculate. Oh what a fury!"

Chablis noticed that she was experiencing a rise between her legs and, as usual, when sexually aroused, her sphincter muscles began contractions. O.K., Dandy Dildo might be evil, but she started to understand its power, as it was even having an effect on her. She found herself desirous of a good pounding, even though she had one that morning from Carlton.

Mr. Martin continued: "with a woman as beautiful, kind, loving and gracious as my mother was, I could have never imagined her doing what she did to my father. Sex is a glorious thing that brings humanity great joy and should be savoured with delight, but in this case, it was pure evil from that damn thing. My mom was like a diamond that sparkles and glows with splendour, and my father showed her the kind of love that should have made her stand like an invincible fortress against those who might tempt her. Each day as he gazed upon her magnificence of mind, body and spirit he realized that she was like the morning sun that glowed brightly on the horizon of hope. Still, that abomination stole their happiness, as she could not resist its power."

"Tell me about how she killed your father."

"It is something that, as a child, I was not completely privy to. However, I know that she and he were having sex one night and she asked him to take out the dildo and use it on her."

"Apparently, as he was trying to use the dildo on my mother, it actually turned on him, began to spurt out a long steady horrendous stream of semen into his face as the police found the bed full of sperm. He nearly drowned in the semen, and my mother sat on his face as he was gasping for breath, pressing hard with her huge ass as she shouted 'lick it baby, lick it.' She sat on his face so hard that she broke his nose as she tried to smother him with gorgeous ass so that he could go to heaven, according to her, and tell St. Peter that he died from too much ass."

As had been the situation often in dealing with this case, Chablis fought back laughter. Mr. Martin could tell she was struggling to contain herself, so he said through laughter, "Go ahead and laugh. It is damn funny, but it is the truth."

They shared gregarious laughter together and as it subsided, Mr. Martin continued. "So, as you can imagine, there was no real enthusiasm for bringing a woman to trial for murder by ass because a dildo told her to do it."

"Yes, I would sympathize with a DA having to prosecute that case. And you, of course, know how your mom died in the asylum? Any idea what happened to the dildo?"

"My mother had hidden it in a deep dark corner of the basement. She told her brother that it had to be gotten rid of as soon as possible, because as long as it was around she or some other woman might be unable to fight the temptation. She loved my father dearly, but she had simply fallen prey to this evil entity that destroyed her completely as she became obsessed with fornicating with that damn thing."

"Her brother knew the story of what happened, so he very carefully took a box to the basement. I remember that he carried a shotgun with him. He put it in the box, took it up to Mermaid Landing and threw it into the lake there."

"Mermaid Landing? Can you give me directions? I want to look at the place."

He gave her directions and escorted her to the door. Chablis gave him a kiss on the cheek and thanked him. He leaned in against her and she actually felt he had an erection. She said, "Why you dirty old man."

CHABLIS AND THE DILDO FROM HELL

He smiled broadly and said, "My wife has been gone for six years. Would you just touch it?"

Chablis was a woman with infinite compassion. She reached behind her and closed the door, dropped to her knees and unzipped his pants. It was only partially erect, but she didn't care.

She blew gently on his passion root in a teasing fashion rubbing her nose through the pubic hair; she eased back and blew upon it like the wind that blows gently on a summer's day. She was starting to drive him wild with anticipation. She was not worried about him having a heart attack, because she knew he was a man of great health and stamina; anyway, what a way to go. She flicked her tongue over the head of his penis. She softly kissed her way down the side of his shaft, slowly and tenderly sucking little portions of it. She was gentle as a feather with her caresses.

She grabbed hold of the base of his member which was now growing to a nice size. She cradled his balls in her right hand, gently massaging them up and down, as she kissed and licked his shaft. Her mouth found its way back to the mushroom-shaped head and she softly kissed it and sucked it into her mouth. "Oh! This is heaven!" he moaned.

No teeth at all, she used only her lips and tongue to caress the tip and she artfully moved slowly up and down, up and down, up and down, slowly sucking more of him into her warm, moist, soft mouth. She glanced up at him seductively with her dark penetrating gaze, looking into his now tearing eyes. He looked down smiling as tears flowed freely down his cheeks. "You have no idea how good this feels," he moaned in a low, soft, pleading voice. But she did know how good it felt, because so many men had shared praise for her cock-sucking abilities, and this one was special for her, so very special.

Her hand was firmly gripping his balls now and the slow moving up and down motion made Chablis feel like she was on a sailboat riding waves in a sea of passion. She eased toward the top and made a gentle suction with her mouth around the head as she slowly and methodically worked from top to bottom, burying her nose in his pubic hair. She loved doing this for him. She thought that this should be part of Medicare – one blow job a month guaranteed by a beautiful woman, and for women, one wild fuck from a young virile man. Age was just a number not a sign on the door that said *life-over*. Sex was a part of good health. It was needed for a good frame of mind.

It kept getting harder and he began to pump back and forth as Chablis gradually increased the speed of her sucking in sync with his pumping motion. She put copious amounts of salvia on the shaft, stopped sucking and held his balls in one hand, lubricating them with her saliva. She began to move her hands in a fashion so that they were alternating – following one after another starting from the head and going down the shaft until she reached big balls. Then she released him – but at the same time as she released the one hand her other hand was holding the head and beginning to slide down his shaft towards the balls. Again, as soon as she got to the base, her other hand was at the head following it down ever so slowly as his tears were stopping now while he moaned.

She took him into her mouth again, just the tip at first, bobbing her head up and down, taking a little more of him into her with each bob going down. Soon she was following the entire length of his shaft with each bob, and started speeding up the pace. She grabbed the base of the shaft with one hand and moved it up and down to the same speed as her mouth was moving up and down on him. The rhythm was perfect now – in total sync. She could sense that he was almost ready!

She then took the head into her mouth and just sucked on it like she would an ice cream popsicle, not moving her head at all, with her hand pumping up and down the shaft and her tongue flicking the head and rolling it around inside of her mouth.

His balls tightened up and the skin drew itself firm. He was ready to blow, but Chablis wanted it to be his best blow ever, so she released the shaft, and while still sucking, she again started to bob her head up and down quicker now. Her hand began rubbing on his thigh as his pants had slipped down around his ankles and he grabbed the back of her head, just playing with her soft hair. Then it came – he erupted into her mouth, squirt after delicious squirt! It seemed like it would never end, and felt so good to Chablis as it gushed down her willing throat making her body go rigid. She slowed down but did not stop the gentle sucking now as she wanted him completely empty. She continued to suck on him, bobbing her head up and down, going ever so much slower every time. Finally she stopped moving her head once again with only the tip of his penis in her mouth, and with a firm grip her hand was once again pumping up and down on the shaft while her tongue was very gently licking the head. He jerked just a bit as she slowly withdrew her mouth, and gently blew on the head. She looked up and he was crying again. She stood up, wrapped her arms around him and whispered into his left ear. "I did it because I wanted to. It was incredible. You owe me nothing, and I will remember this until my dying day. Thank you so much."

He could say nothing as Chablis reached down, lovingly pulled his pants up and took his withered, wrinkled old hands and placed them on his belt, all the while with a sincere smile of genuine affection on her face. He zipped up and she gave him a wink as she turned and walked out the door, leaving behind a man who had just been taken to Chablis heaven.

She was indeed an angel. There were those who would call what she did the very definition of being a slut. The truth was that this act was an act of great kindness that far surpassed any act by so-called Christians who would come pray with him, encourage him to admit his sins and get right with Jesus so that the doors of heaven could be opened for him. Of course, they would also urge him to remember the church in his will so they could use the money to spew more of their hate and vile judgemental arrogance. Chablis was an angel who had just given a blow job that even St. Peter would realize was a true act of kindness in a world where it was in short supply.

CHABLIS AND THE DILDO FROM HELL

CHAPTER 7
WHILE HE LAY THERE IN PAIN

Take a horny woman and give her rhythm.
Eat, lick, penetrate and please rebellion.
Disguised as God, a dildo is selfish desire.
And that Dandy Dildo can set her on fire.

It merges irrationality and reality,
Severing all ties with normal humanity.
Embracing, proclaiming sexual calamity,
Abandoning kin and standing tall,
On an isle of corpses,
Balding trees and forceps
Float on the sickly crimson waters
Of once virginal daughters!

Martyrs to passion's sighs
Of an exasperated lust.
The will to appease, release and please,
The sounds, pontificating against silence
Shattered and battered in defiance,

CHABLIS AND THE DILDO FROM HELL

Taking wild fornicating in lustful alliance,
Lying there waiting not shyly.
There will be quaking and dying.

Aching for ecstasy from it and writhing,
Demanding and legs prying apart,
All that can be done to tickle the heart,
As the wild pounding is about to start.

The battery operated boyfriend that is war;
The revelry you take from sweet pains.
Obtaining from time and white flags wasted,
And basted in carnal juices become useless.

The climax for which so many have waited,
The fated end to tame it,
Heinous amounts of nameless bodies.
Nonchalantly keeping women company,
The bastard that is the beast
Answers women's cries: "Give it to me!"
Wave after wave of delight
Shines each woman with lust's light.

The guns lust stop.
There's nothing left.
Everybody is out of breath.
Blessed are the women with a rhythm.
They shame themselves to come again,
For now that mock all sin.
Here's to your devout rebellion.
Keep that angst from resounding.
Ah, Dandy Dildo finished the pounding!

J. Wayne Frye

CHABLIS AND THE DILDO FROM HELL

Chablis parked her car and made her way up the path to Mermaid's Point. The was an overhang on the right side, the sound of the river raging toward the lake among the rocks, and the dashing of the waterfalls around spoke of a power mighty as omnipotence.

As she ascended higher, the valley assumed a more magnificent and astonishing character. Ruined homes hanging on the precipices of piny mountains and cottages every here and there peeping forth from among the trees formed a scene of singular beauty. But it was augmented and rendered sublime by the mighty mountains in the distance, where white and shining pyramids and domes towered above all, as belonging to another earth, the habitations of another race of beings.

She passed a foot-bridge where the ravine, which the river forms, opened before her, and she began to ascend the mountain that overhangs it. Soon after, she entered the valley. This valley was more wonderful and sublime, but not so beautiful and picturesque as the mountain above, through which she had traversed.

A tingling long-lost sense of pleasure often came across her during this journey. Some turn in the road, some new object suddenly perceived and recognized, reminded her of days gone by, and were associated with the light-hearted gaiety of childhood. The very winds whispered in soothing accents, and nature wrapped her in hope. But why was she going here? What would she find?

There was no gaiety in this place, now deserted and forgotten. This was the place where Leland Martin's uncle had come to toss away that which had come between his sister and her husband. He had tossed the physical object, but the psychological object was never released by his sister. And what was Chablis proving by coming here? What could she find in this dissolute place?

She went to the lake's edge, walked about wondering where Leland Martin's uncle might have tossed Dandy Dildo. Surely, it would have been in a more secluded place. As she was walking about, she noticed a female couple sitting by a tent. She strolled over and introduced herself. They said they had been camping there for a few days. She was asked to have coffee with them which she graciously accepted. Sarah and Jane explained that they had gotten married three days ago and were spending their honeymoon in the loveliest spot they knew. Chablis thought to herself that despite numerous roadblocks to equality, that the USA, one of the most backward First World countries, had finally embraced the right of marriage for all. She found it refreshing that these two had no shame about their love, and that for the majority of younger people in the nation; gay marriage was no big deal.

CHABLIS AND THE DILDO FROM HELL

They spent a wonderful early afternoon talking, and when the girls found out who she was, they were fascinated as they had heard of her, one of them having read Wayne Frye's account of the famous case of the *Terrorist Who Resurrected the Spirit of Che Guevara*. Jane asked if she was on a case.

Chablis recounted the legend of Dandy Dildo and expected them to laugh heartily, but they did not. In fact, they offered an incredibly interesting tale of their own, and below I lay it out for the reader to analyze. It is recounted exactly as told by the two young ladies who shared storytelling duties.

Sarah began. "We are all open-minded women here, so I am going to be a bit crude at times with the story, but here goes. It is interesting that you brought up Dandy Dildo, because our great grandmothers, after heir husbands died, found one another in their 60's and started a torrid love affair with one another. It's been quite some time since we told this story about our grandmothers. We call it *The First Time With a Large Dildo*. It is the evolution after a year together of their fun with that venerable toy."

"Some time, as I said, about a year after they moved in with one another, my grandmother, Louise, purchased a dildo for Jane's grandmother, Kelly. Now, they had one rule about a dildo - the bigger, the better. In this case, not only was it a tremendously large toy, but it also came with a cyber-skin that felt extremely realistic. Rather than a sex shop, it was purchased in an antique store. The truth about this toy is that it was actually too big for Kelly's pussy to accommodate entirely. But she still had some incredible, earth shaking orgasms on it and the two of them used it in unison sometimes."

"The dong measured beautifully long from tip to base, but what is truly impressive was the girth; it went just shy of nine inches around, and was slightly asymmetrical. For comparison, get a soda can and measure it around, then imagine putting it inside your pussy or ass. My point is that this thing was becoming a regular part of their sex routine, but then something strange happened. They got a visit from the man who had sold it to Louise, and he asked if they would sell it back for ten times what was paid, because he had a buyer in Boston who was anxious to have it. They talked it over, but decided that they were enjoying it too much to part with it."

"A few days later, the man interested in purchasing it showed up again. He offered them $5000 for it, saying that he had been fishing near Mermaid Falls almost 2 years before and got it caught on his hook, reeled it in, took it home to his wife, and that he actually became jealous of it and sold it in frustration."

CHABLIS AND THE DILDO FROM HELL

"It had been gone almost three months and he had no peace from her as she simply would not have sex any longer without including it in their play. She insisted what she had come to call Dandy Dildo be returned to her. It seems she had even begun to talk to it on occasion, and he often heard it talking back; although, he assumed it was just her mimicking the voice of a man. He had consulted psychiatrists, and they indicated that getting it back would probably be best in order to quell her deep rooted angst. They sold it to him and that should have been the end of the story, but it isn't."

Chablis, slapping a mosquito off her arm, said "Go ahead, please."

"Well, it seems Kelly simply started having withdrawal pains as she desperately missed the dildo, and although Louise bought several others, none of them would do. So, the two of them decided to go down to Boston and find the owner, a Gretchen Helms. They went to her residence and asked what she would take for the dildo, as they missed it desperately. She laughed in their faces and said, 'you don't sell the Rembrandt of love.' She slammed the door and Louise assumed it was all over, but it wasn't.

At this point, Sarah started coughing, so Jane took over the story. She was more intense than Sarah as she continued the tale. "These two were a bit perturbed, but Louise simply said to Kelly that they would have to accept the fact that the dildo was irretrievable. It was then that Kelly revealed a secret. She told Louise that the dildo was alive. That it communicated with her. Now, as you might expect, Louise was dumbfounded and, at the same time, concerned about Kelly's mental state. Still, that night, as they lay together in their Boston hotel room, the two hatched a plot to steal the dildo from Gretchen Helms."

Again, as she listened to the lengths to which women were willing to go in order to fornicate with Dandy Dildo, Chablis fought back laughter. The whole incredible story seemed to get more outlandish with each passing day.

Jane continued. "So, they knew that the dildo would be in use that night as the Helms couple made love. They crept up to their bedroom window and just peeked in, figuring that the two would make love using the dildo, put it aside and go to sleep, at which time they would go to the patio door in the back, use a glass suction tapper to cut a hole in the glass door, unlatch it, slip in and retrieve that which had become an obsession to Kelly. However, all did not go exactly as planned. As they were watching the two make love, they themselves became overwhelmed with passion. They began to passionately kiss and fondle one another. As they were doing so, they heard a commotion in the bedroom."

CHABLIS AND THE DILDO FROM HELL

This commotion was caused by what Louise assumed was the ventriloquist skills of Gretchen Helms, for they stood in shocking awe at what they heard. As her husband was jamming the dildo into her derriere as she rode his member, a male voice, obviously not Gretchen's husband's kept singing:

In the centre of a golden valley,
I dwell in darkness divine,
A pretty creature's ass is all mine
In pleasure I festively dine.

Oh my darling, oh my darling,
My darling hot ass divine,
I am lost in here forever,
But the darkness is divine.

Your husband is a foreman
Of your pussy hole mine,
And everybody knows they can
Dive into this whore divine.

Oh, this slut loves a sixty-niner,
In dreams and thoughts sublime,
Lives in comfort with her dildo,
waiting for lust's sign.

Many others often pray
But in this dark clime
Lust is the prayer for her,
This favourite nugget on which I dine.

J. Wayne Frye   113

CHABLIS AND THE DILDO FROM HELL

When the day is done and there is setting sun
Its rays they cease to shine,
Homeward comes a husband
To caress and lick his gold mine.

None is nearer, none is dearer,
As the days of sixty-nine
He knows he must share with another
A dildo by Karson so fine.

.

This slut's lust is like a river,
The weather in her is fine,
She is a tasty morsel not a sliver,
Her dark chamber is a gold mine.

Oh my darling, oh my darling,
Oh my darling so sublime
In you I am lost and quiver forever,
Damn bitch so fine.

Drove into her deep and hard
Every morning and every night,
Oh she let loose her sphincter,
And I fell in and outta sight.

I love pumping in her canyon,
Where the darkness does entwine,
Her pussy smells so fine
But on her ass I dine.

In the centre of a golden valley,
I dwell in darkness divine,

CHABLIS AND THE DILDO FROM HELL

A pretty creature's ass is all mine
In its pleasure I festively dine.

"The two of them could not believe the feverish sex escapade they had witnessed, as it appeared all over, as the dildo seemed to literally unscrew itself from Gretchen's now gapping hole. It rolled off to the side as the two lovers lay exhausted from their carnal frenzy, but Dandy Dildo was not through. As the husband lay face down on the bed, it jumped upon his ass and quickly bored its way in, pumping furiously as the man helplessly lay moaning grotesquely from the pain while his wife laughingly said, 'ram him hard Dandy, ram it like there is no tomorrow.' She was in a delirious tantrum of unfettered evil desire shouting, 'fuck that bitch, fuck him.' She rose and started jumping on the bed, up and down, up and down. She rolled her husband over and cocked his legs up, straddling him as Dandy Dildo continued his pumping. She bent his legs back so far you could hear bones cracking as she let out a steady stream of urine into her husband's face, so much that he began to gag. She was drowning him in it. As he struggled for breath, the two heard an evil proclamation from Dandy Dildo that was muffled by the depth it was in his ass, but the words were clear. It said laughingly, 'drown him with your piss bitch, I want to fuck a dead man.' Oh, where all the urine came from was amazing, but she gushed it forth like a tsunami roaring ashore on some island in the Pacific."

J. Wayne Frye   115

CHABLIS AND THE DILDO FROM HELL

As had been the case so often, Chablis simply could not hold back the laughter. It burst forth slowly at first and then it cascaded into a crescendo. Suddenly, Jane and Sarah also began to laugh, but through their laughter, Jane said, "It is true, according to our grandmothers. Funny yes, but you have yet to hear the whole story."

Chablis, her laughter subsiding, said "Go ahead and continue please."

Jane continued in earnest fashion. "So, they stood and observed in complete fear as they felt if they were to intercede that dire circumstances might ensue. They watched helplessly as Gretchen's loving husband paid the ultimate price for his love. He drowned in urine, and as he took his last breath, Gretchen was shouting, 'fuck me Dandy Dildo, he has been fucked to death, let me join him in the delirium of sexual heaven too.' And Dandy Dildo did. Our grandmothers watched in horror as Dandy unscrewed itself from the ass and leaped upward into Gretchen's mouth. The damnable thing fucked her mouth so hard and so furiously that she collapsed onto the bed and as Dandy squirted a huge stream of cum that gushed out the side of her mouth, she choked to death in a flood of cum that was of Biblical proportions. As she lay there dead, Dandy pulled out, and with cum still squirting from its slit, looked over at the window. The slit at the head crept into a sinister smile."

J. Wayne Frye

CHABLIS AND THE DILDO FROM HELL

Sarah interjected "And what it said haunted the two until their deaths. It did not scream, but rather whispered softly, 'You bitches ready for Dandy Dildo? I'll give you lesbians the pounding of your lives and make you die with a smile on your faces. And when you get to the pearly gates you can tell St. Peter to flap his wings and come on down so I can fuck him like Satan in heat.' The two of them ran like a couple of scared rabbits. The next day they read in the paper that there was an unusual joint suicide in Boston as a man and wife had apparently killed themselves in a sex ritual. No details were given, but our grandmothers shared the details with us often. They never used a dildo again, as they were simply too frightened after what they saw."

Chablis, interested by the tale, but by no means convinced of its validity, said "And you genuinely believe your grandmothers saw this?"

Without hesitation, they both replied, "We do."

"Well, I admit that I have accumulated some interesting details, and it appears that coming here in search of this dildo was a wasted effort, but meeting you two confirms that it is obviously no longer in the river here. So, nothing was ever heard of it after that as far as you know?"

Sarah replied, "Nothing except there were some strange occurrences that they followed closely."

CHABLIS AND THE DILDO FROM HELL

"What occurrences?"

Jane, in a serious tone, shared what she knew. "Well, all across New England many strange things happened in regards to deaths from what were generally categorized as sex rituals. This went on for many years but has died down the last 10 years I would say. One of the strangest occurred about 10 years ago right here near Brattleboro."

Sarah interrupted. "Yes, the strangest of all I would say."

Jane, very emphatically, continued. "It happened in an old house outside Brattleboro. There was a family called Monahan. There was the father, the mother and two very attractive daughters aged 18 and 20. The two girls were the most sought after two in the whole area, as they simply glowed with incredible beauty, but the father kept a close eye on their suitors.

"The two girls were known to be a particularly wanton, but had to be as discreet as possible because of their father. He kept a very watchful eye on them both. One day he caught the girls in the woodshed fornicating with two young men. The boys were nearly killed by Mr. Monahan. Now, this is important to remember because of what happened later on. You see, the boys were so severely beaten that they required hospitalization."

CHABLIS AND THE DILDO FROM HELL

Sarah offered an addendum at this point. "You see, this is important because of what Mr. Manahan was accused of doing about one month later. Although he was a strict man who adhered to severe punishment for his daughters if they strayed from what he deemed the righteous path, he was not completely ignorant like most religious paragons of virtue. He realized that women their age were obviously interested in sex. Wanting to make sure that what occurred never happened again, he set off for Boston, as there are, as you might expect, no adult toy stores in Brattleboro. He went to buy dildos for the girls, and while he was in an adult shop, according to the account he gave the police, a man noticed him looking at the dildos and told him that he had the world's most unusual dildo. When he told him that he needed two for two different girls, the man said that this dildo could simply be washed and shared as it was the ultimate pleasure giver. He said it would be expensive, but that he would gladly allow his wife to demonstrate its value. So, Monahan, who was actually titillated by the thought of watching a woman use a dildo on herself, gleefully went with this man to his home. When he got there he was warned that the dildo had the power of speech and that it had actually been invented by a man named Karson who had lived near Brattleboro. Now, Monahan had heard about the Karson family and the wild tales of his fantastic invention, but he had always scoffed at the stories as nothing more than fantasy. He was about to discover they were true."

CHABLIS AND THE DILDO FROM HELL

"He was introduced to the man's wife who was named Celeste. She was a cute thing with huge breasts, a shapely body and lusciously provocative lips. She and her husband were swingers and said they would love some fornicating pleasure with Mr. Monahan as threesomes were their favourite sexual escapade. Now like so many people who profess religious fealty, it seems Mr. Monahan talked about high moral standards, whatever they are, but when it came right down to it, he was just like everyone else. If hypocrisy could be bottled and sold, the religious virtuous finger pointers could make a fortune. Anyway, it seems they all got naked very quickly and started what would be a wild evening of pleasure. Now, what happened next is speculative perhaps, but it is what was told to the police by Mr. Monahan. As they were enjoying wild fornicating pleasure, the man reached under the bed with his right hand and brought out what he called Dandy Dildo. It seems that Celeste was busy sucking Mr. Monahan while her husband was licking Monahan's balls and Celeste was riding her husband's cock. The man flipped the dildo on the end of the bed. Suddenly, Monahan heard a devilish voice say, "Ass ramming pleasure on it's way. I'll ram you so hard up you shute I'll tickle your belly button with the tip of my cock. So enthralled with the blow job he was receiving while his balls were being licked, Monahan simply ignored the voice, but Celeste began sucking him furiously as she kept bucking backward to meet the strokes from the rear."

J. Wayne Frye

CHABLIS AND THE DILDO FROM HELL

"Monahan had a mind-blowing ejaculation into Celeste's willing mouth. She let his cock pop out and started shouting, 'Dandy I am randy for some scrumptious semen from your hard tool. Pump me baby, pump me hard.' It was then that Monahan heard a voice that echoed like it was coming from inside a tunnel. It said, 'Dandy do, Dandy did, Dandy can. It is dark in here but it is my home. Ram your hubby so hard he blows his load like a hopping toad. I will match him double for his load. Get ready for a flood that will drown you in cum.' So mind-blowing was the man's orgasm that he let out a scream so loud that the ceiling cracked and debris fell onto all of them. Celeste was hit in the head by the falling light fixture over the bed just as she exploded in orgasmic ecstasy. She was killed instantly, and collapsed onto her husband as he had a massive coronary from the force of his orgasm. His last words were 'open up the gates of hell devil. Here I come with a smile on my face.' Somehow, Monahan managed to survive the ordeal and noticed a huge flood of cum seeping out of Celeste's ass. Dandy Dildo suddenly popped out, and Monahan swore that the slit in the mushroom head smiled at him. He grabbed Dandy Dildo, went to the kitchen, put him in a plastic bag and quickly left the premises, not reporting the deaths for fear of what it would do to him and his reputation. Only later, when he was in police custody, did he reveal the truth about how he came by Dandy Dildo. He drove back home with the dildo by his side. It was a mistake!"

CHABLIS AND THE DILDO FROM HELL

"Keeping quiet about how he came by Dandy Dildo, he called his daughters and wife into the living room and sat them down. He told his daughters that he understood that they were maturing and needed to satisfy certain urges. He reached in his plastic bag and there it was – Dandy Dildo. They all gasp at its size. He said that the two girls were to share it as it was special and would bring them many hours of pleasure. He suggested they alternate nights using it. He noticed that his wife was eyeing it with intense interest, but said nothing. The first two nights the girls alternated using Dandy Dildo and the parents were astounded at how vocal they were when using it. Obviously, it was serving its purpose. Now, the two girls went to the Brattleboro branch of the University of Vermont days, so the mom was left at home while Mr. Monahan tended the farm. Overcome with curiosity, the mom slipped into one of the girl's rooms and borrowed Dandy Dildo. She went to her bedroom, lay down naked and started to slowly insert it into her vagina. She felt a warm glow she told her husband later and it seemed to take on a life all its own as she did not even have to work it back and forth. It started doing that itself and she heard guttural sounds of pleasure emanating from it. Then she was shocked when some disembodied voice said, 'you fucking bitch. You are tighter than your slut daughters. I'll make your hole so wide a Rolls Royce could park in it.' She was shocked, but so delirious with pleasure she just kept enjoying the pounding."

J. Wayne Frye

CHABLIS AND THE DILDO FROM HELL

Her husband came in and caught her enjoying Dandy Dildo, but was so turned on, according to his police deposition that he pulled out Dandy and dived right in himself. However, as they lay on the bed in delightful afterglow, they noticed that Dandy Dildo was slowly working its way toward Monahan's wife's pussy. He reached down to grab it and a voice blurted out, 'Don't touch me bitch. I want a woman today. I'll fuck your ass tomorrow.' In shock, Monahan said to his wife that the thing was evil. She responded that it might be evil but that it gave her the best sex of her life and she wanted more. He got so angry that he reached down to grab Dandy and throw it away. However, the slit in the mushroom head opened wide and swallowed his hand. It held it in a death grip and as he pleaded for it to let go his wife kept saying, 'kill the asshole, and we'll fuck on his grave.' Again, according to the police deposition, he became so enraged that he reached for the base of the dildo, pulled his hand out fighting to get out of his grip. He finally tossed it against the wall just as his daughters came home from school and immediately heard the commotion, rushed to their parent's bedroom and upon seeing Dandy Dildo on the floor, started shouting obscenities at their parents for messing with their lover. The younger daughter then said to her sister, 'he is my lover. He loves me, not you.' Suddenly they started fighting each other over the damn dildo. The father leaped up to intercede, but Dandy Dildo got behind him and started screwing him in the ass."

CHABLIS AND THE DILDO FROM HELL

"The wild pounding was so furious that Monahan fell to the floor unable to ward off the deadly assault. Meanwhile, as he lay begging Dandy Dildo to stop, his wife had gotten up to try and intervene between the daughters who were by now flailing away at one another. In the process, the mother was knocked back against the wooden foot of the bed, crushing her skull and leading to instant death. The two sisters continued to battle as Dandy fucked away shouting 'kill everybody bitches, kill them all and we'll fornicate furiously in the church aisles at their funerals.' Monahan was desperately trying to get up to no avail. As he looked on in horror at his wife lying dead on the floor with blood gushing out of her head and his two daughters continuing their frantic fight, he felt helpless as Dandy continued to ram him like a wrecking ball pounding an old building into oblivion. The older sister managed to slam the younger one against the wall, hitting her head so hard the younger girl crumbled to the floor unconscious. Mr. Monahan pleaded with his daughter to help him as Dandy Dildo continued the wild sexual frenzy only to be told by her that he was getting what he deserved for messing with her lover, whom she would one day marry when it became legal for dildo and woman to engage in nuptials."

Again, Chablis burst out in laughter, but Sarah said, "What is funny about a man being fucked to death by a dildo while his daughter watches?"

CHABLIS AND THE DILDO FROM HELL

Chablis said, "I am sorry, but you have to admit this is farcical at best."

Sarah replied, "O.K., O.K., you are absolutely right of course, but get ready to really laugh at the next grotesque part of the tale. Go ahead Jane finish it."

Jane seemed eager to continue. "O.K., this is as reported by Mr. Monahan to the police when he tried to explain things. So the dad was being pulverized by Dandy Dildo while his daughter leaned over her mother and tried to pull off her right arm shouting that she was going to use it to beat her sister to death so she could have Dandy Dildo all to herself. She went to the kitchen and came back with a butcher knife, according to Mr. Monahan. Now, remember this is all simply what Mr. Monahan said happened, but there is no independent verification. Anyway, Monahan is lying on the floor helpless as he watches his daughter cut off his wife's right arm, and all the while Dandy Dildo is in complete delirium laughing crazily as it continues pounding away. The older daughter manages to sever the arm and just as the younger sister wakes up, she starts wailing away with the severed arm, beating her into submission until the young girl expires from a series of blows to the head. Apparently all this activity has sexually stimulated the older sister, so she starts begging Dandy Dildo to please pull out of her dad and fuck her. Dandy suddenly blows a huge load in the father and leaps over to the older sister."

Chablis said, "Wait, wait a minute. This is the most preposterous story I have ever heard. Monahan must have been a lunatic. Who would ever believe this wild tale?"

Jane said, "That is the point, nobody did. But let me finish the tale. So, according to Monahan, as he lay on the floor, struggling to get up, Dandy was wilding ramming his daughter so hard and so furious that he feared for her life. He struggled to his feet, but just as he was about to try and pull Dandy out of his daughter's vagina, the daughter kick up with her left foot and hit him in the groin while shouting, 'don't you dare, I'm going to orgasm to death and love it, fuck me Dandy, please fuck me to death.' Well, as Monahan lay on the floor writhing in pain from the kick to his balls that is exactly what happened. His daughter, even according to the coroner's report, was literally fucked to death. Of course, Monahan was arrested for the murder of all three and declared insane. End of story."

Perplexed, Chablis said, "Not completely. What did he say happened to Dandy Dildo?"

Sarah, shaking her head, replied, "According to Monahan, Dandy Dildo just started rolling out of the bedroom while he lay there in pain."

CHAPTER 8
GODZILLA WAS A PUSSYCAT

We rest, but a dream
Has power to steal sleep.
We rise, but wondering
Has power to pollute the day.

We feel, conceive and reason.
We laugh and we weep.
We embrace happiness, but deceit
Has the power to take it.

Whether it is joy or sorrow,
The path of its departure is free.
Man's yesterday may never
Understand the power of his tomorrow.

Shattered pines with needles of doubt were scattered within Chablis' mind; the solemn silence of doubt was broken only by the brawling waves of commitment to her cause. The thunderous roar of the avalanches of laughter at the ridiculousness of the case seemed to bury her in hilarity. Still, her commitment to the scientific method of detecting elevated her from all littleness of feeling, and although it did not remove her doubt of authenticity, it subdued and tranquillized it.

Each night she fornicated with Carlton, but her thoughts were often of his father, who had somehow touched her heart as well as her body. No mention was ever made of their sexual escapade that night, but each day they bonded with conversations of depth where the old man's character titillated her mind as well as her body.

As day broke one morning, rain was pouring in torrents, and thick mists hid the summits of the mountains in the distance. Despite the hilarity of the whole matter, she wanted to penetrate the misty veil and seek whatever truth there was to the case of Dandy Dildo. The ridiculousness of it all seemed to grip her, pull her ever farther into the growing despair over the fact the case was beyond any stupidity she had encountered before, but there was still that element of doubt that seemed to mock sanity. Was, somewhere within the incredible ridiculousness of it all, a small thread of truth?

She felt that somewhere in those ruins, somewhere on that old estate was a key that would open the door to the real truth about Dandy Dildo, and with that in mind, Chablis set out for the Karson estate.

As she roamed the estate, she felt a path to truth was somehow about to dawn. The path was littered with ravines of doubt, but a luxuriant light of hope always burned within Chablis. That was her nature. Why, she thought, does man not boast of sensibilities superior to the base desires that trap him? As long as impulses were motivated by greed, man might never be free; for man was moved by every wind that blows and a chance word or scene that a word may convey. Truth was out there beckoning, but how could she find it? How could she fight through all those stories that were, no doubt, embellishments and somehow arrive at the truth?

> *Wandering spirits,*
> *Do not rest in your narrow beds.*
> *Allow me this faint pursuit of truth.*
> *Take me, as your companion,*
> *And show me the light.*

For some time she sat outside the ruins of the mansion. A mist seemed to engulf her and all that was about her. Suddenly, on a ledge of a small hill to her left, an oblong object seemed to be slowly rolling about. Its rolling motion was smooth and determined. She perceived, as the shape came nearer, that it was the dildo of which she had heard so many horror stories.

CHABLIS AND THE DILDO FROM HELL

She trembled, not with rage, but excitement. It approached; its countenance bespoke bitter anguish, combined with disdain and malignity, while its unearthly ugliness of intent rendered it almost too horrible for human eyes.

"Abomination of evil," she shouted at it as it stopped no more than a few feet from her.

"Why, what an unfriendly greeting" it whispered in a voice that seemed to come from the fiery pits of hell. It stopped, tilted slightly toward her and a slight smile seemed to crease the slit in the mushroom head. "I can mesmerize most, but you my little wretch of wantonness I sense cannot be mesmerized by Dandy Dildo, for you are already free of any restraints sexually. You know pleasure has no boundaries and live a life free of shame. Your purpose is to kill me. I am beyond your petty deeds, though. I am immortal. I shall eventually fuck your wanton ass as if it was jelly in a bowl of desire."

Chablis could not believe she was actually conversing with a dildo. Was she dreaming? "I seek not your demise. I only seek to corral your evil and bring you to him who has employed me."

"Seek the truth arrogant bitch. You know it not, for he who has employed you is more evil than I. Be wary of those who deceive with dicks of desire. You fornicate him and are blind. Be calm!

CHABLIS AND THE DILDO FROM HELL

Life, although it may only be an accumulation of anguish, is dear to me, and I will defend it for I am conceived of pleasure by the mighty Dr. Karson who spawned me. Remember, he made me more powerful than himself; my sexual prowess is superior to all before and all that might come after. I am the perfect pleasure machine. Bring me not to he who would destroy me, destroy the glory of my existence for pleasure. Surely, a woman as free-willed sexually as you are can understand the cravings for pleasure? Everywhere I bring bliss. Even in death people cling to me, because I deliver on a promise of grand delirium. I am benevolent and good; on a person's last breath I deliver on pleasure as people embrace the darkness simply because of the joy I deliver."

"You destroy all that you touch."

"It is destruction that they embrace."

"Will nothing I say make you have a favourable opinion of me? So, Karson's servant brought him the brain of a killer, the veins of a soul trapped in mental illness. Is that my fault anymore than it is the fault of he or she who is birthed by a woman whose genes are corrupt? Is it the baby's fault that it is a product of heredity? My creator abhorred me and it was he who was my creator. Where can I find refuge? For ten years I have lived here among the ruins of my heavenly home, as I grew weary of the world out there."

CHABLIS AND THE DILDO FROM HELL

Chablis, still aghast that she was conversing with a dildo, said, "Come with me then. I shall not hand you over to Carlton Broughton. I shall find you a place where you can know peace."

"These bleak days are not to be sublimated my sweet. If the multitude of mankind knew of my existence, they would demand my destruction. I am seen as an abomination when all I want is to fuck, fuck, fuck. It is in my nature, planted there by the Dr. Frankenstein who created me. For example, right now I long to pound your sweet ass like a pile driver slamming into rock. You see, I have grown to hate all, hate all who see me as a pleasure tool and cannot comprehend that I am capable of love if only given the chance. I am miserable, and want all to share my wretchedness."

Chablis, still not convinced that she wasn't hallucinating, said light-heartily, "Is there no hope for you? Have you never found a woman or man with whom you have true simpatico?"

"Do not be flippant with me bitch. Let your compassion be moved, and do not disdain me. Listen to my tale; when you have heard that, abandon or commiserate me, as you shall judge that I deserve. But hear me out. You have only heard one side of the story filled with falsities, misconceptions and innuendo. The guilty are allowed, by human laws, bloody as they are, to

J. Wayne Frye

speak in their own defence before they are condemned. Listen to me, who has lived the misery of only seeking pleasure and nothing else. You accuse me of murder no less, and yet you would destroy me without trial, because I am a lowly dildo. Listen to me, and then, if you can, and if you will, destroy the work created by Karson who set-out to make me because of the love he had for his young wife."

"Am I to pity you Dandy Dildo who has wrought destruction upon so much humanity?"

"Can you not have the courtesy to hear my side? Listen to me and grant me compassion. Hear my side; it is long and strange. Hear my side and decide. On you it rests, whether I quit forever the neighbourhood of man and leap into the river that flows near here and stay submerged for all eternity or perhaps you could pity me, and show me some love, make me your lover or at least keep me safe in a drawer in your home where the dark can become my friend as I know someone had compassion."

Still not sure she wasn't in a fantasy world, Chablis said, "I shall lend you my ear fiend." She looked upward toward a clouding sky and continued, "But it appears rain is again eminent. Let us go inside and make ourselves safe from the elements." Oh, Chablis was so wise, as her aim was to have him let down his guard.

CHABLIS AND THE DILDO FROM HELL

As they moved toward the ruins of the once palatial estate, she weighed the various arguments and she determined that she owed Carlton Broughton nothing. He could have her fee back. All she wanted now was retribution and an end to the horrors of Dandy Dildo. However, he was a wily fornicator and had killed before with unexpectedness. She knew that she must be on guard, because he was indeed a worthy adversary.

The air was cold, and the rain again began to descend. They entered the ruins, both with what seemed heavy hearts and depressed spirits. However, Chablis had consented to listen, and seating herself in a remnant of a wooden rocker by what had been the fireplace, she nodded her head at Dandy Dildo as a way to encourage him to begin. Thus, began Dandy's side of the story.

"My dear beautiful maiden, it is with considerable difficulty that I remember the original era of my being; all the events of that period appear confused and indistinct. A strange multiplicity of sensations seized upon me as I was born, and I saw, felt, heard, and smelt at the same time as I became alive. By degrees, I remember, a stronger light of warmth pressed upon my nerves. Though I could not see, the brain I was given let me seem to always be able to visualize in my mind. Darkness then came over me as time passed and troubled me, but hardly had I felt this when, by visualization, as I now suppose, the light of my

J. Wayne Frye

reason for being poured in upon me. I could not walk but I rolled with precision. The brain my creator gave me made me desire to pound, pound, pound again and again into an alluring ass or pussy. Time passed for me and I now found that I could wander about at liberty, not needing to see with eyes, but with my brain. You, no doubt, know of how I was introduced to my creator's wife and she became enthralled with me. This roused me from my nearly dormant state, and I ate the forbidden fruit again and again. Oh, how tasty it was."

Chablis found his method of relating his woes interesting, but she still had to fight back laughter as there she sit, listening to a dildo. She began to think that maybe it was like one of those remote control devices kids played with, those things that were vastly overpriced in Radio Shack or some other electronics stores. Yes, maybe this was a conspiratorial joke being played by a group of people who wanted to shame her. No, no, that was not possible. She let the thing continue.

"Imagine having been dead? Well, my various parts that is had been dead. I felt cold inside, and as it were, instinctively, finding myself only designed for pleasure. I wept. I was a poor, helpless, miserable wretch; I knew, and could distinguish nothing; but feeling pain invaded me on all sides. I was born with desire to pound, pound and pound men, women, even animals. My life depended on it I reasoned. I feared death without pounding."

"Soon, a gentle light stole over the heavens and gave me a sensation of pleasure as time flowed on. I enjoyed the warmth of my creator's wife's pussy and ass, but I told myself there must be more. So, I left in search of adventure. The huts, the cottages, and stately houses engaged my admiration. I decided to enter one of the cottages, but I had hardly placed my foot within the door before the children shrieked, and one of the women fainted at seeing a talking dildo. The whole village was aroused; some fled, some tried to attack me. Why oh why I asked, for I am but a lowly dildo that means no harm. Why are they repulsed by me? I escaped to the open country and fearfully took refuge in caves up on remote somewhat inaccessible Mermaid Mountain. In the end, I found no agreeable asylum from the misery of being an outcast among some, and only an object of desire by others. I had everything some would say who countenance sexual pleasure as the ultimate in life, but beneath my desires that were engrained in me by my creator, I was a mere empty shell, an empty dildo filled with nothing but a mountain of cum also fostered by my creator to make me pump into women that which they desired so wantonly. I tell you I curse my creator, curse him for giving me so much ability to sexually satisfy, but when it was over, I felt empty inside and used."

CHABLIS AND THE DILDO FROM HELL

I lived a solitary existence in my cave, fornicating with animals on occasion, because my desires were too strong to curb. One day I beheld in my mind a young creature, with a pail by her side, passing before my cave. As she walked along, a young man met her, whose countenance expressed a deeper despondence. Uttering a few sounds with an air of melancholy, he took the pail from her and bore it to a nearby cottage. She followed him inside. I heard wild guttural sounds of fornicating frenzy. Oh, I was aroused and wanted to pump either one of them really good. I wanted; no I needed some fornicating action."

Chablis looked down at her dress where there was a slight indention between her legs and she could feel she was on the rise. My, oh my, she was aroused by Dandy Dildo.

He continued his story. "So, I visualized the fornicating frenzy and when they got into a roaring 69, I elected to dive into the woman's generous ass. At first she apparently thought it was his finger being inserted, but soon she felt my girth, but assumed he had somehow miraculously produced a dildo as she said, 'oh baby, shove it in – it tickles so good, but it is so huge.' He became mystified as he reached around and felt me pumping back and forth on my own. His words horrified her when he shouted, 'it ain't me babe. That dildo up your ass ain't me I'm telling you.' She screamed like a banshee in the night."

CHABLIS AND THE DILDO FROM HELL

"I did not stop pumping, and I slowly squeezed completely into her ass and then she said to her lover, 'Hey, this thing's good. What am I scared of? Umm, pump my dildo lover, pump.' Her boyfriend became enraged and told her this was sick. She was replacing him with a dildo. All she could do was shout 'fuck it baby. Fuck it good.' Her boyfriend climbed out from under her and reached down for me, but I said, 'don't touch me bitch, I'm fucking.' He was in shock that a dildo could talk.'

As was so frequently the case, Chablis simply could not hold back her laughter as she burst out in a hilarious uproar only to have Dandy Dildo say, "This is serious shit bitch. Stop your laughing."

Getting some control of herself, Chablis said, "I'm sorry. It is just that I have had to suspend reality lately to try and understand this, but here I am talking to a dildo, so why I am laughing I do not know. This whole case is preposterous."

"Preposterous? You want preposterous? I'll give it to you. Get ready bitch. So, here I am indulging in my sole purpose in life – fucking, and this hot bitch I'm humping tells her boyfriend to take a hike as she is finally getting fucked by a real cock, not a puny piece of meat like the one he has. He gets so enraged that he starts pissing on her and she just says, 'um baby, it's so warm, please don't stop.' O.K., the boyfriend is pissed – how's that for a pun? Anyway, he cuts off in mid stream, walks over to the kitchen table and picks up a knife. I can sense it of course and visualize it with ease but I am too busy fornicating to care, as all I want to do is keep pumping this bitch until she explodes like Mount Vesuvius in ancient Rome. Just as she explodes with a mind-blowing orgasm, he plunges the knife into her back once and all she can say is 'damn, I'm dying with a dildo up my ass.' He plunges again and again as I blow my load into the bitch's ass, pull out and as he is stabbing again and again, I squirt a load in his face. He turns to come after me, and I roll like a road runner onto the floor and out the cabin door. I am too fast for him, but I have had enough of the chase, turn to face him and tell him that I'll drown him in cum. He rushes toward me and I start gushing my liquid gold. It is so furious and so much that it halts him in his tracks. He drops to his knees pleading, 'stop cumming, stop cumming.' However, I am the one pissed now, so I keep squirting it in his face until he lies on his back drowning in it as I stand over him and keep cumming and cumming and cumming. Damn, how I love to cum and my creator made it possible for me to cum and cum and never stop. I was born to cum, but I usually prolong it for self-satisfaction, but I am really upset with this cretin who kills his girlfriend simply because she prefers a quality fuck from Dandy Dildo to his tired old way of giving it to her."

CHABLIS AND THE DILDO FROM HELL

"It was at this time, as he lay dying, a young girl, not beautiful but cute, comes by and looks down upon the now dead man and says, 'wow, you dildo ejaculated all that cum? You must be the Karson phenomena? I heard about you from lots of women who say you are the best. They all loved your flood of joy juice. Got any left?' Now, I never like to see a maiden in distress, so I simply said that I always have a steady stream ready for a fair maiden like her."

"I went back to an old cottage with her and she introduced me to her father who was blind. She simply told him that I was her friend and she wanted to invite me in to hear him sing. The old man, with his guitar, produced sounds sweeter than the voice of the thrush or the nightingale. It was a lovely sight, even to me, poor wretch who had never beheld such music before. The silver hair and benevolent countenance of the aged cottager won my reverence, while the gentle manners of the girl enticed my love. Not lust notice I said, but love. He played a sweet mournful tune which I perceived drew tears from the eyes of his amiable companion, of which the old man took no notice, until she sobbed audibly; he then pronounced a few sounds, and the fair creature, leaving her work, knelt at his feet. He raised her and smiled with such kindness and affection that I felt sensations of a peculiar and overpowering nature; they were a mixture of pain and pleasure, such as I had never before

J. Wayne Frye

experienced, and I, myself whimpered in the corner, unable to understand these emotions. The young woman was occupied in arranging the cottage, the old man got up and walked toward his bedroom, leaning on the arm of the young woman. Nothing could exceed in beauty the contrast between these two excellent creatures. One was old, with silver hairs and a countenance beaming with benevolence and love; the younger was slight and graceful in her figure, and her features were moulded with the finest symmetry, yet her eyes and attitude expressed the utmost sadness and despondency. Night quickly shut in as the girl helped the old man to bed. He said goodnight to me and thanked me for coming by, and encouraged me to spend time by the fire with his daughter who longed for male companionship besides him. I could sense the hint of his hope that I would fornicate with her so she would know the delight of sex. Oddly, my thoughts were not of sex for the very first time. I was filled with wonder that someone could be so nice and as accommodatingly kind as these two.

"This lovely woman sat with me and not once mentioned sex, but rather only said that she sensed I was troubled by the misery of my situation being born for pleasure only without the attachment of love. She dwelled on the grand things in life that were not sexual, but reached the heart of each individual in pursuit of life's meaning. The two of us fell asleep as we conversed."

CHABLIS AND THE DILDO FROM HELL

This thing, this creature created for lust was beginning to tug at Chablis' heart strings. She found herself sympathizing with a murderer.

He continued his story. "What chiefly struck me was the gentle manners of these people, and I longed to be part of something I knew nothing of – family. I remembered too well the treatment I had suffered from the barbarous elements that only wanted me for pleasure. However, I resolved on that night now 10 years ago to put aside my hatred of mankind and pursue peace rather than pleasure. Still, they were not entirely happy as the young woman would often go to her bedroom and I would hear her weep. After a week, I had not fornicated with her and fought any such urge as I did not want to rush things. Soon, I discovered one of the causes of the uneasiness of this amiable family: it was poverty, and they suffered that evil in a very distressing degree for I come to realize in America people are blamed for their poverty as if it was a preventable disease. I had many discussions with her about how they were ostracized and looked down upon because of their plight as if they could really do anything about it. Their nourishment consisted entirely of the vegetables of their garden and the milk of one cow. They often, I believe, suffered the pangs of hunger very poignantly for several times she placed food before the old man and she reserved none for herself. I, of course, needed no food, so I was a perfect guest."

J. Wayne Frye

CHABLIS AND THE DILDO FROM HELL

The rain stopped and Chablis sighed. The dildo had grown more comfortable with her and continued his story. "This trait of kindness moved me. I had admired this young woman's grace and one night, after her father had gone to bed, she received a gentleman caller. Not wanting to cause trouble, she told me to hide in her bedroom. As the night wore on, I found myself getting jealous of her time with this young man. There was a mirror on the back of her door, and as I rolled toward it and looked I realized that I must appear hideous to her and to all others, but they all wanted me for pleasure, not looks. They all wanted to just use me. Hatred began to swell up within me, hatred for all those who looked with disdain on a lowly dildo that just wanted some love, some compassion, some understanding. I stared at myself and felt the pangs of disappointment for my slavery to lust. In turn, I reflected upon the perfect forms of my hosts; their grace, beauty and delicate natures. I was in reality a monster, and I knew it. I was filled with the bitterest sensations of despondence and mortification. Yet, I did not entirely know the fatal effects of this miserable life my creator had given me."

"I became part of the family, and the father, who had still not deduced I was less than human, began to grow especially fond of me, and finally he said that it was time that I and his daughter shared a bed, as she was of age and needed the love of a good man."

CHABLIS AND THE DILDO FROM HELL

"The first night I slept with her my thoughts were of gentleness not unfettered pounding. I worked myself into her chamber of desire and gently fucked her. She moaned with delight, and for the first time I got pleasure from sex not just lustful satisfaction. Each day found me discovering the motives and feelings of these lovely creatures. I began to feel it might be in my power to bring them some happiness as they were such deserving people. I looked upon them as superior beings who would be the arbiters of my future destiny. I formed in my imagination a thousand pictures how my young maiden named Felicia and I could reveal to her father that she was in love with a dildo. I imagined that he would be disgusted. I lived in fear that somehow their family or friends might show up and I would be found out, but she always managed to hide me. Still, I could sense her father growing suspicious that something was amiss."

"My mode of life was becoming normalized. My spirits were elevated by the enchanting appearance of nature; the past was blotted from my memory, the present was tranquil, and the future gilded by bright rays of hope and anticipations of joy. However, one day, as we were all sitting around enjoying some music from the old man, an ill wind in disguise pulled up in an old pick-up truck. He was a grand looking young man who asked for directions to the old Karson estate. My dear love and I were outside but I hid in the woodpile as she conversed with him. She gave him directions and then asked if he would like to come in for a bite to eat, which he did. I rolled out of the woodpile and leaped into the bedroom window where I hid listening to the conversation. Doing so made me contemplate my fate in life. I was simply too abnormal to saddle this lovely young woman with a lifetime of living in the shadows of polite society. After all, how could a dildo and a human legally marry? Oh, how I longed to just be normal, to maybe figure out a way we could have a family, but my sperm was sterile. Yet, I had visions of adopting, but how could I do that to a child. How would the child feel introducing a dildo as his father? How awkward to say, 'here is my lovely mother and this is my cum-spurting, pussy-ass pounding father – the dildo.' No, it would never do. I was doomed to a life of loneliness."

His seriousness was adding to the jocular nature of the whole thing. Chablis actually looked around, suspecting that there must be a hidden camera somewhere. Surely the whole thing was a set-up engineered by the Broughton family and she would find herself signing a release so the whole stupid thing could be shown on television. As she glanced around, Dandy said, "You witch. You do not believe a thing I have said. Can you not feel just a little bit of my agony? Are you so heartless as to have no sympathy for my miserable plight? Surely, even a lowly dildo is entitled to a bit of compassion."

CHABLIS AND THE DILDO FROM HELL

"I am sorry, so sorry, but you have to understand that this whole affair seems absolutely fantastic, beyond belief. I am a practical person, and I have seen the original Frankenstein movie. It is as if this whole affair is just like the movie. I apologize, but talking to a dildo is not my normal every day routine."

"You think this isn't normal. You have no idea woman. I am capable of destruction as you could not even imagine, and I am almost at the end of my rope after all these years lying dormant, building up my reserve of cum and desire to pound. Godzilla was a pussycat compared to the damage I can do."

J. Wayne Frye

CHAPTER 9
THE DILDO FROM HELL

Pardon sweet flower of matchless poetry,
And fairest bud the red rose to ever bare;
Although my muse is in deeper care
Presents thee with a wanton elegy.
No blame my verse of loose unchaste,
For painting forth the things that hidden are,
Since all men act what I declare,
Complaints and praises one can write,
And passion-out their lyrical rhymes,
But of love's pleasures none did ever write
Any more grand than of Dandy Dildo times.

It was the merry month of February
When Dandy Dildo became contrary.
Ah, he danced about with glee,
But there were few who could see,
Or taste the cream of his good cheer,
Because he had bred so much fear.
Still, he had built a lustful shrine.

CHABLIS AND THE DILDO FROM HELL

And made so many women his valentine.
He looked about for some hot ass
On any fine and randy lass.
Thither went he to boldly inquire
If any hot woman would light his fire.

Oh, Dandy Dildo was hotly accursed
To quench passion's thirst.
All about was a bevy of females to decide
Which one he would first ride.
A lass named Francis caught his fancy there.
And he pounded her without a care.
And his fever she would not debate,
For her orgasm was of highest rate.
Dandy Dildo rang her bell,
And he wanted all her to tell,
For he was on a fornicating rampage.
Hey, he was lust's fine sage.

Others lined up all around,
For once again Dandy Dildo was found
They all knew he was the best,
So they filled out a request.
Come one come all from hither.
They'd fuck him shine or stormy weather.
Pretty maidens were there to behold,
And Dandy would never get old!
Ah, wombs were waiting to be filled,
And there was Champaign to be chilled.
And bearing it all in naked delight,
Ah, the girls were an incredible sight,
As Dandy Dildo each pussy did strike.

J. Wayne Frye

CHABLIS AND THE DILDO FROM HELL

Dandy was the new rage all about
As orgasm after orgasm was so stout.
All women with him were content,
For they felt he was heavenly sent.
Now Dandy was one to keep,
Because he could pound so deep.
Inside puss or ass he was askance,
With lust's piercing pounding lance.
Sweet women had been forlorn
But with Dandy they were reborn.

You see with Dandy there was never a pause,
Because he was 100% devoted to the cause.
He put each maiden in deep bliss,
As his mushroom head they'd kiss.
He never ceased to astound,
While passion he unwound.
His technique was smooth as silk,
And he loved to squirt his milk.
He pleaseth and sprayeth with verve,
As he struck passion's nerve.
He had a deep reservoir of cum,
As everyone he wanted to give some.

He loved each and every hole,
For his creator gave him a fucker's soul.
One night a woman lay when he was done,
And she said she wished she could give him a son.
He said I give you many thanks,
But I'm here to fuck your shanks.
I need absolutely nothing more,
So go to sleep you wanton whore.

J. Wayne Frye   149

CHABLIS AND THE DILDO FROM HELL

Dandy pounded them each and every one,
And he was devoted to getting the job done.
He had no eyes to see their countenance shine,
But on pussies and asses his mind did dine.
He was carved from pieces with lascivious wit,
And his pounding would absolutely never quit.
What else can be said of his devotion to the cause?
This dildo that from duty would never pause.

Fighting back laughter as always, Chablis asked Dandy to continue with his story of woe, promising not to be so dismissive of his tale. She was still sceptical, but she had been hired to find Dandy Dildo and was now conversing with him, but still formulating her strategy for getting him to Broughton.

You could sense that Dandy was suspicious of Chablis, and he rolled slightly away from her, perhaps in anticipation that she might try to grab him. He had great powers of will to manipulate people, but he knew that Chablis was less susceptible than weaker minded individuals. His story was indeed captivating, even if the whole thing was a farce, though Chablis did listen intently.

"I learned that the possessions most esteemed by your fellow creatures revolved around riches. Without wealth, in this nation, you are nothing. This is a nation that worships at the altar of money."

CHABLIS AND THE DILDO FROM HELL

Chablis nodded her head in agreement as Dandy continued. "Of my creation and creator I was absolutely ignorant, but I knew that I possessed no money, no friends, no property. I was, besides, endued with looks that satiated a person's desire for pleasure, but beyond that I was a physical abomination to be laughed at. I had been imbued with great agility by my creator who wanted me to be able to sexually satisfy even the most demanding of partners. I bore the extremes of heat and cold with no injury to my frame. When I looked around I saw and heard of none like me. I could have no dildo friends because none of them were given life as I was. They were just inanimate objects with no feelings. Was I, then, a monster, a blot upon the earth, from which all men fled and whom all men disowned? Perhaps to most men yes, but to women I was a God, but a God of what? I was only a God of pleasure but to my dear Felicia that is. Still, I cannot describe to you the agony that these reflections inflicted upon me; I tried to dispel them, but sorrow only increased with knowledge. And all the while my love for the dear Felicia grew, but what life could a lowly dildo offer such a fine lass? My pain grew, even as I enjoyed a modicum of happiness with her. I wished sometimes to shake off all thought and feeling, but I learned that there was but one means to overcome the sensation of pain, and that was death, a state which I feared yet did not understand. I admired virtue and good feelings and loved the gentle manners and amiable qualities of my two new friends, but I was shut out from polite society, and while many ridicule and belittle those who practiced hedonism, almost all harbour the same desires they degrade. Hypocrisy was the norm of that day and today."

Chablis leaned forward and with sympathy said, "Hypocrisy I know well, because as a transgendered woman, I have been approached for sex by many who would reproach me in public and scold me as an abomination."

"Then we have something in common I suppose. Many a good church going Christian woman who would speak with disfavour on sexuality had no problem riding old Dandy for hours on end when their husbands were away. Anyway, I had settled in well with the family and the old man liked me I could tell. Yet, I could sense that he was concerned that I was never around when someone visited. I looked at these good people and could barely recall the distant evil that seemed so much a part of my past. I felt that time was done for, because lowly, demonic-like Dandy Dildo had somehow found love."

"By reading to me nightly, Felecia fostered in me an infinity of new images and feelings that sometimes raised me to ecstasy of a completely different type than to that which I had been born into and grown accustomed to. The gentleness she displayed pleased me so much. Still, each night as we lay in bed I asked her why she could love such a useless creature as me. She always responded that to her I was more than a dildo. I was the light of hope for her, giving her more than conjugal blissfulness, but deeper, more meaningful understanding and companionship that no one else had ever offered. Were it not for the disdain and rebuke it would give me, and for the lack of compassion from a Catholic Church that would never agree to it, she would marry me and let the whole world know that I was so much more than just a dildo."

Despite the seriousness of his tone, it was all Chablis could to do to hold back laughter. She had never been so thoroughly inundated with the absurd in a case before. Yet, in spite of it, here she was conversing with a dildo. She was not so sure she shouldn't' check herself into a mental institution.

"One day, my love departed on a long walk, leaving me behind. The old man took out his guitar and began to play a mournful tune. You could see his thoughtfulness and sadness as he played the Hank Willams' tune *I'm So Lonesome I Could Cry*. At length, laying aside the instrument, he sat absorbed in reflection. My heart palpitated as I knew my hour of trial was about to occur. My hopes, dreams and fears were about to be laid bare. There was silence all about us; it was foreboding; yet, I was almost welcoming the coming tribulation as my parts went weak and I sank into despair. The old man said to me that he knew that I was Dandy Dildo of Karson fame and that though others had forgotten me for years and I was assumed long gone that he knew, despite his blindness, that I was the one who had been among them for so long now. I was the one who had stolen his daughter's heart, and that it was partly his fault for encouraging the union, but when he had done so he had no idea that I was the Karson creation. He saw me as a kind and caring dildo, but that, for his daughter, he had to find better. She could not live life with a dildo as her husband. It simply was not fair to her. Deep silence ensued. I knew that every minute was precious to me, yet I remained irresolute in what manner to commence my defence. I told him of my pain in being friendless, alone and only sought for pleasure until I met him and his daughter who showed me kindness and affection that I had never known."

"He said that he understood my pain and that I should always have the two of them as my friends. He said that he had heard of my evil, but to him and his daughter he had seen nothing but kindness from me. However, he felt that I should seek out my own kind, find another dildo and maybe the two of us could find comfort with one another, but I told him that I needed a hole to bang and a heart to love, not another one of my kind who offered nothing but companionship. I longed for; I needed without reservation, love."

CHABLIS AND THE DILDO FROM HELL

At that instant the cottage door was opened, and Felicia stood there staring at us. She knew that her father was aware of the secret. She did not have to be told. She sensed it. I started, for the very first time, to cry. She ran to me, dropped to her knees and kissed my beautiful mushroom head, saying that she loved me, turned to her father and pleaded with him not to make me go. I rolled to her father and in silence whimpered as a new born child. In a transport of fury, he arose and furiously started to stomp on the ground, trying to crush me. Felicia shouted that I should run, run from him and his fury, because he could not understand the love of a woman for such a kind, caring dildo as I."

"I left my beloved as I cursed my creator and what he had wrought. Why did I live? Why, in that instant, did I not extinguish the spark of existence? Why did I not roll to the nearby cliff and fling myself into the river? I knew not any hope as it had all been dashed in an instant when the bigotry of dildo hate reared its ugly head; despair had not yet taken possession of me; but my feelings were those of rage and revenge. I could with pleasure have destroyed the old man, but my love for Felicia restrained me."

"I gave vent to my anguish in fearful hatred. I was like a wild beast that had broken the toils, destroying the objects that obstructed me and ranging through the woods with a stag-like swiftness. Oh! What a miserable time! The cold stars shone in mockery, and the bare trees waved their branches above me; now and then the sweet voice of a bird burst forth amidst the universal stillness. Oh, I needed to pound, pound, pound and pound any hole, anywhere, any time with fury."

"I, at that very moment, declared everlasting war against humanity, and more than all, against him who had formed me and sent me forth to this insupportable misery. I was raging in fury at my creator, my God who had forged me."

"Into the woods frolicked a young maiden of maybe 20. I calculated to get her for pounding. I was no longer a kind and caring lover. I was about to unleash a fucking fury as the world had never seen. I was about to become the dildo from hell!"

CHAPTER 10
HELL HATH NO FURY LIKE THAT
OF A DILDO SCORNED

He prepared to drown in fornication,
And pound away his pain.
Ah, Dandy Dildo was on fire
And about to go insane.

Dandy was once again randy.
For in mighty pursuit of pleasure,
He did not tarry for long,
As fornication was his treasure.

He had been rebuked by the old man.
Ah, sweet Felecia had never said goodbye,
But now he had a rising fury
That he could not let lie.

Ram, ram, ram in fury.
He was on a wild rampage,
About to unleash hell,

CHABLIS AND THE DILDO FROM HELL

For too long held in a cage.

Look out fair maidens about.
This dildo was not to be denied.
He was filled with growing hate,
And his lust could not be defied

Dandy now seemed to boil with fury as he continued his tale of how he was again scorned. "I continued to roll through the forest until I came to its boundary, which was skirted by a deep and rapid river, into which many of the trees bent their branches, now budding with the fresh spring. Here I paused, not exactly knowing what path to pursue, when I heard the sound of voices that induced me to conceal myself under a log. I was scarcely hid when the aforementioned young nubile girl came running towards the spot where I was concealed, laughing, as if she ran from someone in sport. She continued her course along the precipitous sides of the river, when suddenly her foot slipped, and she fell into the rapid stream. I rushed from my hiding-place and rolled into the water so she could use me as a life-raft. She managed to get to shore and was aghast that a dildo had saved her. She stroked me with affection, but I needed pussy or ass and I said, 'give me some puss or ass babe for a reward.' She was shocked to hear me talk, but she was curious when onto the scene the person from whom she had playfully fled appeared. On seeing me, he darted towards me, and hastened to try and stomp on me. I sprang onto my balls, stood tall and started to squirt my joy juice in copious amounts into his face. Oh, but he was carrying a rifle and he aimed it at me. He grabbed her by the arm and fled as she shouted, 'hey it's just a dildo, you two can double fuck me. Let's give him a try.' But alas he uttered, 'that is the evil dildo of Karson fame. He has returned. Hurry, least we fall prey to its evil.' They scurried away and gone was my chance to pound."

"Once again, my kindness was abused. I saved the bitch's life. The least she could have done was give me one good fanciful frolic. This was then the reward of my benevolence! I had saved a human being from destruction, and as recompense I now writhed under the miserable pain of being called an abomination. The feelings of kindness and gentleness which I had entertained before gave place to hellish rage and gnashing of teeth. Inflamed, I vowed eternal hatred and vengeance to all mankind. Revenge, sweet revenge on humanity would be my new order of business."

"As my fury raged, by the stream where I lay a beautiful child of maybe 10 approached. Suddenly, she gazed upon me, and obviously knew not what I was. An idea seized me that this little creature was unprejudiced and had lived too short a time to have imbibed a horror of my deformity. If, therefore, I could seize her and educate her as my companion and friend, I should not be so lonely. I put aside my fury again."

CHABLIS AND THE DILDO FROM HELL

"As soon as she beheld my form, she placed her hands before her eyes and uttered a shrill scream; I said, child, what is the meaning of this? I do not intend to hurt you; listen to me. Still she was repulsed by me. She said, 'Ugly wretch! You wish to fuck me and tear me to pieces. You are an ogre. I will tell my papa.' I began to cry, for I meant her absolutely no harm. She was but a child, and though I was built for pleasure, I was not a pedophile. I had no designs, no lust for a child. I would never stoop that low. However, I knew if she told her father, the woods would be filled with gun-toting cretins looking to destroy me. I mean this is America where guns are as common as apple pie – more common than apple pie. I was afraid."

Chablis had done her research well. She said, "You killed the child. I read in the papers that she was apparently tossed over a cliff by her assaulter."

"No, no, I never did that. Listen and hear what really happened. You read an article in an old paper that was fabrication not fact. She started to run from me, and she was headed toward the precipice over the river's edge. I shouted to her, but she kept running, so I rolled quickly in front of her, trying to keep her from running over the edge. In the process I blocked her way, digging my big balls into the earth and pleading with her to stop. She didn't. She tumbled over me into the gorge below. The investigation was hushed up, because they found the imprints of my giant balls in the earth. What were they supposed to tell the public – *giant dildo kills child?* The rumours were already rampant about the Karson creation and they feared mass hysteria. They frantically searched the forest for days and days as I hid in fear. I slipped back to see Felicia, and she welcomed me in tears, saying she knew that the paper was all lies and that the authorities were after me, and she knew I would never harm a little girl. I replied that I could no longer tolerate the hatred and that I was about to explode in a frenzy of fury and mayhem. She pleaded with me to stay, but I told her there was no hope for us that she needed to find her a human to love, because falling in love with a dildo offered no hope.

"As I left her home, I ploughed through the forest in a frenzy of vileness. I came across a sheriff's deputy who gave me no respect. He fired shot after shot at me as I rolled through the area like a giant rolling pin of fear. I led him into the forest, finally hiding in a tree branch and when he came under it I pounced on him. I flailed away at the back of his neck until he fell to the ground. As he struggled I subdued him with a flurry of cum that nearly drowned him. He let lose his hold on the gun and I tore through his pants, finding his hole where I plunged in and started pumping, pumping with such a fury that he begged me to stop as he could take no more. I didn't stop."

CHABLIS AND THE DILDO FROM HELL

"I gazed on my victim, and my heart swelled with exultation and hellish triumph; clapping my balls as if they were hands, I exclaimed, 'I ram you with fury bitch and dispatch you to hell where I have lived since my creation. Welcome to my world.' Then I cut lose with so much cum that the poor slob simply collapsed with fear. He died of fright."

"As I fixed my eyes on the carcass, for a few moments I gazed with delight as my rage would not subside. I remembered that I was forever deprived of the delights bestowed on people like those who looked upon me with disgust. Can you not understand my rage? I only wonder that at that moment, instead of venting my sensations in exclamations and agony, I did not rush among mankind and perish in the attempt to destroy them all. While I was overcome by these feelings, I left the spot where I had committed the assault, and seeking a more secluded hiding-place, I entered a barn which had appeared to me to be empty. A woman was sleeping on some straw; she was young, and blooming in the loveliness of youth and health. Here, I thought, is one of those who uses joy-imparting smiles to get some of me, then discards me once pleasured. And then I whispered, 'Awake, fairest, awake and get rammed by Dandy Dildo, the finest fucker in the land.' She opened her eyes, saw me and immediately pulled down her panties, spread her legs and cried for me to ram her hard and furious."

CHABLIS AND THE DILDO FROM HELL

"I rammed her with such a fury that she exploded in a mind-blowing organism that nearly ripped the roof off the barn. Afterward, she did not rebuke me but begged for another ramming, rolling over on her stomach and giving me her ripe ass. Oh, I gave it to her so good that she nearly fainted from the pleasure. Still, she did not rebuke me, but lay there thanking me as she had not had such a good ramming in ages. She pleaded with me to visit her girlfriends so they could know the pleasure of a real fuck, but again, I saw that I was only for pleasure. Well, I rolled between her legs and gave it to her again for good measure and she was so delighted she lay there in blissfulness afterward as I rolled out the barn door and headed for my next fuck of fury."

Dandy went quiet and sighed. Chablis sat bewildered, perplexed, and unable to arrange her ideas sufficiently to understand the full extent of talking to a dildo in a case that was quickly making her grow more leery each second. Was it time for her to throw in the towel, tell Broughton that this whole thing was a colossal mind-fuck and just walk away? What was to be gained, anyway? It was only money and she and Aaron had plenty of cases on the burner to supply that. Yet, there was something still driving her, still making her want to see this thing through to the end. Even though Dandy was a murderer, she found him pitiful, as he was a creature that had been born for pleasure but never really got any himself.

CHABLIS AND THE DILDO FROM HELL

The mountains in the distance seemed majestic and strange, and there was a misery, a melancholy hopelessness to the place where Chablis sat conversing with a dildo. How could a sympathy-laden Chablis assist this lowly creature in assuaging his inner turmoil? How could she help put his soul in harmoniousness simpatico with humanity? Was it even possible? Chablis' wild and enthusiastic imagination was chastened by the sensibility of her heart. Her soul overflowed with ardent affections, and a devoted wondrous nature fuelled a desire to reach out with hope.

She trembled as she looked down upon the silent Dandy. A ghastly grin suddenly wrinkled the slit on the mushroom head. He had loitered in forests, hidden himself in caves, taken refuge with one he grew to adore, but in the end all was lost, for he had no one, no place and no hope. As Chablis gazed in silence upon him, his countenance expressed the utmost extent of malice and treachery, but still she harboured sympathy for his plight. Dandy, without word, rolled away into the twilight of the day. He disappeared around a corner. Chablis felt for her snub-nosed 38 but did not withdraw it to blow the dildo to smithereens. She remained there, gazing into the now growing darkness. The winds were hushed, and all nature reposed under the eye of the quiet moon. She felt the silence, although she was hardly conscious of its extreme profundity, until her ear was suddenly arrested by a noise off to her left.

J. Wayne Frye

CHABLIS AND THE DILDO FROM HELL

She pulled up her dress and fondled the 38 in its thigh holster. She trembled not from fear but from anticipation. She had a feeling of helplessness so often felt in frightful dreams, when you in vain endeavour to fly from an impending danger, but are rooted to a spot. Presently she heard the sound of gentle footsteps and there stood Carlton Broughton. He stepped before her and said, "You found it didn't you?"

Without hesitation, she replied, "I did."

Excitedly, he replied, "Why, why didn't you get it?"

His manner made her realize that there was far more to this than was being revealed. She said, "I didn't get it because it was an inopportune time. He had me at a disadvantage."

"Then you have spoken to that abomination?"

"I have, yes, and I must admit some sympathy for the thing. He has been much maligned, and though that may not excuse its behaviour, there are mitigating circumstances."

Chablis was seeing a side of Broughton with which she was unfamiliar. His calm, kind, caring demeanour was evaporating into a raging fury of tyrannise discontent as he shouted. "Maligned, bull-shit. It is a devil looking for victims."

CHABLIS AND THE DILDO FROM HELL

Chablis, shocked, said, "OK, let's settle down and maybe it is time for you to tell me the truth about his whole sordid affair. Level with me. I can't serve a client who lies to me."

The darkness hid some of Carlton's frantic facial expressions, but Chablis knew he was frightfully dismayed. He eased over toward an old wooden box, sit down with his head in his hands, sighed, looked up and said, "I am sorry. I lied to you, because, well, to be honest, I am ashamed of the truth."

Chablis, perceptive detective and astute observer of the human psyche that she was, said, "Your mother was with Dandy Dildo."

A look of shock overwhelmed Carlton. "Yes, but how do you know?"

"I'm a pretty perceptive person. That's why I am such a damn good detective. It fits now. Obviously, you are filled with hatred, because apparently this damnable thing came between your mother and father at one time."

"I was a child, a young child when my mother was taken from me, taken, not by death as all thought, but by insanity – insanity caused by that damned thing."

"Tell me the whole story. Spare nothing."

CHABLIS AND THE DILDO FROM HELL

He let out a long, agonizing sigh and said, "It is dark and cold. Come, I'll drive back to the house. You follow me please dear Chablis, and we'll sit by the fireplace and I'll tell you the whole sordid story."

As they sat by the fire, there was a pall of silence, until Carlton began his story. "There is a time, an hour, a place that is set in the destiny carved out for me. In that hour I should die and at once satisfy and extinguish this malice that hangs over this home that is nothing more than a place where misery has dwelled for far too long. The prospect of death does not move me to fear. You see, I think of my beloved mother, and the endless sorrow that befell this place when she could find no happiness without her lover that barbarously destroyed her and the happiness that once dwelled here. I resolved as a child not to fall before this family's supreme enemy, Dandy Dildo, without a bitter struggle. You see, I saw, as a child, great joy between my mother and father. Their love was the stuff of legends, no less. I saw the intensity of that love and it was transposed to me, their only child who was the product of that love. Ah, but into this happiness of the grandest light snuck a thief in the night and from my father and I that cretin of calamity stole the most precious of diamonds and treated it as if it was nothing but a lump of coal. You have seen my father as a tired old man, but I know he lusts after you, because he lusts after all women, but not for the reasons you would think.

CHABLIS AND THE DILDO FROM HELL

He still seeks my mother in all women he pursues. I know of the little tryst between you two, and I begrudge him or you not one iota, because you did it out of kindness, and he did it because he still longs for the touch of the one woman who made his life complete, but who was stolen from him by that abomination created by Karson."

Chablis, never one embarrassed by sexuality, did bow her head in a slight moment of shame, for she did not want Carlton to think her recklessly wanton. Still, he did recognize her kindness was a motivating factor, but she elected not to completely reveal that it was physical attraction as well as kindness. "Do not think I am quiet so noble, Carlton. Like you, your father is an attractive and appealing man."

Smiling, Carlton said, "Well, I will not ask you who is the more appealing. Anyway, you are too kind to not lie in order to spare my feelings."

Chablis smiled back and said, "I am a sexual woman, very sexual, and men are what I use to scratch the itch of desire that beats profoundly within me. I am neither perfect nor imperfect, just a human being who sees nothing wrong in the free exercise of the sexual urges which are a natural part of our humanity. It is something to be celebrated and embraced, not looked upon with disfavour or disdain. That said, please continue your story."

CHABLIS AND THE DILDO FROM HELL

Fortunately, Chablis sensed that as the night eased on, and Carlton's feelings became calmer, if it may be called calmness when the violence of rage sinks into the depths of despair, as he was now in a better frame of mind to unravel the mystery for her. He sighed and said, "You see, I was always peeping in on my parents, and a few times I caught them in sexual dalliances, which they were never ashamed of. They just stopped and told me that I must always knock when entering their bedroom, because adults did certain things that children should not see. I was a precocious child and, of course, still did my little peeking on occasion without their knowledge. One night, my father brought out this huge cock that seemed to be pulsating with life. He told my mother that he had discovered it while walking near the old Karson place and that it was, no doubt, the instrument that had been the subject of much conversation. He asked her if she wanted to play with it, make it part of their sexual ritual for one night. My mother giggled like a little girl, which was her way of saying yes. Well, I watched my father use it in her vagina while he gave her anal penetration and my mom was, no doubt, in pure ecstasy. I thought little about it, but as time went on, I noticed my mother would slip off to her bedroom often during the days when my father was not around, and I would slip there and observe her using that abomination for her pleasure. What was even stranger was that she actually talked to it, and by some miracle, it talked back to her."

CHABLIS AND THE DILDO FROM HELL

There was a time when Chablis would have scoffed at the absurdity of a talking dildo, but after all, she, herself, had just recently been conversing with Dandy. Consequently, she did not question Carlton's veracity. He continued. "Each day her sojourns with that damn thing got longer and longer, and I watched as she and my father would often argue when she pleaded to include it in their sexual play. He began to see that damn thing as a rival. And I began to think my mother must be a ventriloquist of sorts, as the dildo never talked with my father present. I was too young to understand at the time, but had I been older, I would probably have considered her insane up to a point. Each day things seemed to deteriorate further between them as she became distant and had no time for my father. Then, Dandy Dildo disappeared. I assumed my father had disposed of it, and many years later, he told me that he took it to the Comstock Forge in Brattleboro where he gave it to a friend to toss into the blast furnace, but he didn't. My mother was so despondent over losing Dandy that her mind slowly deteriorated and she became more and more distant, not even caring for me. All she did was sit in silence crying uncontrollably over the loss of Dandy. It finally got so bad that my father had her committed to a mental institution. To save the family name from shame, a story of her death on a trip to Europe was concocted and all were told she was buried there. She died three years later in a mental hospital. Her remains lie in an unmarked grave here."

J. Wayne Frye

CHABLIS AND THE DILDO FROM HELL

How much pain had been wrought, thought Chablis, by Karson's incredibly despicable invention? What started out to be a fanciful lark to bring pleasure to a beloved wife wound up destroying life after life, and even Dandy's own life had been destroyed in the process. Chablis got up, walked over to Carlton, sat down at his feet, crossed her legs, looked up and smiled at him as she placed her right hand on his left leg. She rewrote an old Hank Williams tune in her mind and recited it to him.

Hear that lonesome whippoorwill
That old Hank used to sing about
Remember that the bird was too blue to fly
And like him I can hear the midnight train
Oh, it is whining so blue and low
Right now, I'm so lonesome I could cry

It is a night like his that is so long
When old Hank tugged at the heart
'Cause he realized time can just crawl by
And that the bright moon can go behind clouds
And hide its light from the world
Even the moon can be so lonesome it can cry

Hearing your woes would make a robin weep
Old Hank had his troubles too
That's why he wrote the song he did
When leaves had started to die
He had lost the will to live
Because he was so lonesome he could cry.

CHABLIS AND THE DILDO FROM HELL

The silence of a falling star
Old Hank sang about long ago
That was the star that lit up a purple sky
Now, like Hank, we wonder where we are
Because our lives are asunder
We're so lonesome we could cry

Yes, that lonesome whippoorwill
Is whining over the damage by Dandy
That made so much happiness fly
Like a mournful whistle on a midnight train
That whines so blue and low
Karson's evil has made many cry

Chablis was now determined to end this misery as best she could. Carlton reached down and pulled her up to him. They passionately kissed, and were suddenly on the floor, rolling around on the Persian rug that graced the cavernous room. Clothes were tossed off all across the room in haste as passion took hold and their mouths danced in an open fury with tongues darting about like a flock of geese scared by a gunshot. Chablis rolled Carlton over and reached down to masterfully stroke his member, making it grow stiff and large as she mounted him with her perfectly curvaceous ass swallowing up his member in one full swoop. As it was buried deep within her, she began her rambunctious ride of unrestrained wantonness. Each thrust downward was met by an equal thrust upward from Carlton as they both moaned in harmonious lustful delight.

J. Wayne Frye

CHABLIS AND THE DILDO FROM HELL

Carlton pumped his load up into her and he felt the cum trickle down his shaft and onto his pubic hair while Chablis moaned a low hum of humped delightfulness as she settled her ass down on his now softening rod. She bent over and kissed him, gently rolled off and you could hear her cavity and sphincter relax having obviously greatly expanded from the ride of pleasure. She reached down and gently stroked his softened rod while nibbling on his left ear. She whispered, "I love fucking you."

As his cock hardened again, he whispered, "Suck it baby. I know you love sucking cock."

Chablis winked at him and said, "Does a duck love water?"

Carlton laughed as she worked her way down to his now rising member. It was still warm from the fantastic frenzied fuck she had just given him and she loved its hotness. She devoured it like a person who had not eaten in a week. She pulled it in her mouth all the way to the base, kept it deep down her throat and began to practice a suction technique that was worthy of a patent in the U.S. Patent Office. Not moving up and down, but using suction only, made Carlton moan in ecstasy. She knew she had him completely within her power, as she then began the rhythmic up and down technique combined with her suction motion. Up and down, up and down, suction and more suction had the man writhing in delight.

CHABLIS AND THE DILDO FROM HELL

Carlton whispered, "Oh Chablis, oh, oh, oh, don't stop!"

The explosion was like a tonne of TNT bringing down a mountainside. His joy juice flowed like a river raging in fury down to the sea. Its sweetness hit the back of Chablis' throat with a bang as she gobbled it up like it was the elixir of life.

All the while, by the partially opened window was an observer of the mind. Yes, Dandy Dildo was there to listen to the two wild fornicators and formulate his plans to eliminate them before they eliminated him. The war between dildo, Carlton and Chablis was about to begin in earnest. Dandy had no doubts that his very existence now depended on the elimination of those two. He felt his pleas for compassion from Chablis had fallen on deaf ears, and she and Carlton would both know hell hath no fury like that of a dildo scorned.

J. Wayne Frye

CHAPTER 11
IT WILL DESTROY YOU

On the park bench in the starkness
Of a city facing darkness,
A lady was drinking, feeling tipsy,
Thinking about her life.
Close by was something lurking;
Suddenly it started jerking,
and it seemed that it was twerking!
How could she contemplate
"Will you stop!" She bellowed,
"I am contemplating."
But it jerked incessantly.

She was reaching now her limit,
But it acted like a dimwit,
Covered up by nearby bushes.
What it was she had to see!
The thing came into her sight.
Oh my what a grand light.
It was Dandy Dildo pumping away.

CHABLIS AND THE DILDO FROM HELL

Contemplation was now replaced with lust,
As she watched its girth grow with each pump.
Oh, between her legs was a passionate bump,
As having that thing she knew she must.

She sees the dildo moving.
It was like the thing was grooving.
But to what could it be grooving,
With no beat or melody?
What it heard, she was not hearing.
In the shadows she stood peering,
Wondering if it was leering.
How could she possibly contemplate,
If that thing was leering at her?
Still it jerked incessantly,
And made her wet pleasantly.

Though her heart was filled with dread,
Boldly, she spoke up and I said,
"You there, like some kind of pervert,
just how crazy can you be?
Show yourself. Why are you irking me?
Are you wanting a fuck or a suck?
For what reason are you lurking?
Damn I am hot for a fucking.
Come on you demon, I know you.
Come out of the bushes.
Give me my due."

Finally, she got much bolder.
She walked right over
To those bushes where Dandy hid.

J. Wayne Frye

CHABLIS AND THE DILDO FROM HELL

Oh, what she felt made her dripping wet now.
She lay on the ground and pulled up her dress.
Panty-less, she was now in distress.
"Ram me Dandy Dildo, ram me but good!"
Ram her he did with all his might.
He was starting his rampage to lure Chablis.
He left the poor maiden almost bleeding,
And soon Dandy would have Chablis pleading.

The police report the next day simply said a woman had been sexually assaulted in a Brattleboro park, and apparently the battering was so furious that she was hallucinating and murmuring unintelligible gibberish about some sex toy. However, Chablis knew exactly what happened. Dandy was on the loose. She told Carlton to come with her to the Karson ruins, for that would be where the trail might be picked up. He was instinctively drawn to that place as it was the only real home he had ever known. After all, it was his place of birth.

The irony was that Dandy was expecting the two, and his plan was to lead them on a chase that would prove that he was more than just a fuck toy. He was a wily adversary to be reckoned with. Chablis and Carlton walked about like restless spectres. Their nerves were agitated, but they still maintained a quiet calm as they searched about.

Carlton, looking at an indention in the rocker as if something had been on it said, "Look."

CHABLIS AND THE DILDO FROM HELL

"That's where I sat the other day," offered a smiling Chablis as she added, "my ass leaves a lasting impression."

Nothing could be more complete than the alteration in feelings that had taken place in Chablis in regards to Dandy. Her sympathy had been replaced with disdain for what he had done in the park that night. She looked down on the ground and saw what appeared to be an area where something had rolled over the ground. They followed the indentations for about 1000 metres until they stood by the lakeside. The area was perfectly solitary save for one small boat that was docked and as they looked into it there was a sign, a sign left for them by Dandy. There in the bottom of the boat were two broken twigs forming a V pointing in the direction of the far shoreline and in the distance they could see a boat sailing toward that shore. It was Dandy.

The two, without hesitation, hopped aboard and sat sail following the distant boat. But why, why was Dandy doing this? The sky became clouded, but the air was pure, although chilled by the northeast breeze that was then rising. Clouds hid the now appearing moon, everything was obscure, and they heard only the sound of the boat as its keel cut through the waves. The wind was high, and the waves continually threatened the safety of the little skiff. At all times, they continued to gaze at the little boat in the distance.

CHABLIS AND THE DILDO FROM HELL

They eventually noticed the boat had made it ashore, and Carlton said, "We've lost him."

Chablis said, "No, we will not lose him. He is luring us into a trap. This is his final stand. He is a dildo with one purpose now. He sees us as standing between him and his complete freedom. He is leading us – to where I do not know, but we are on our way to the ultimate showdown."

They arrived on the far shore of the lake in the early morning, looked in the sail boat that had been used by Dandy and saw a trail left by ball dragging on the ground as apparently no longer was he rolling but was skipping about upright, no doubt his giant mushroom head glistening in what was now the rising sun.

As the two cautiously approached a hillside, they noticed it was surrounded by maybe one hundred people. As they stood among the crowd someone shouted, "Strangers, arrest them, take them to the station."

A uniformed officer approached them as the crowd moved aside to expose what was causing all the commotion. There, lying on the ground was a woman, her legs spread wide and a sheet covering her bottom torso. A huge pool of blood had formed between her legs and was coagulating as the crowd shouted. "Arrest the man and take her along too, as his accomplice. They are perverts."

CHABLIS AND THE DILDO FROM HELL

Chablis said, "What is wrong. How did this woman get this way?"

Some old woman offered an explanation. "She was fucked into near oblivion."

"You will know that soon enough," offered the policeman with a hoarse voice. "Maybe you have come to the wrong place to practice your perversions this time."

Both of them were disconcerted on receiving the frowning and angry countenances of the hostile crowd of villagers. This was not Mississippi where you would expect an angry mob to string up anyone perceived as foreign elements in the land, but Vermont, where one assumed cooler heads would prevail. However, the site of a woman who, so ungraciously, had been fucked to near death and was now babbling incoherently, was apparently cause of intense alarm, and why not Chablis thought. After all, Dandy when randy, could leave devastation in his wake.

The policeman did not cuff them, but pointed up the hill and said, "Go, we need to visit Captain Hardy at the station." He had his hand precariously on his revolver as he said it, though common sense kept it holstered as this obviously was not the too often typical American cop who shot first and asked questions later. They marched up the hill as the crowd hissed with displeasure.

J. Wayne Frye

CHABLIS AND THE DILDO FROM HELL

They followed their conductor in silence and were led to the one room police station. Little did they expect the calamity that was in a few moments to overwhelm them? They were introduced into the presence of the captain, a man of maybe 55 to 60 with calm and mild manners. He looked upon them, however, with some degree of severity, and then, turning towards the officer, he asked if he simply brought them in because they were strangers in the village. He replied, "I did, yes."

The captain said, "I apologize for an appearance of rudeness, but an assault is a rarity here about, as are strangers. And we are all shocked at the circumstances as the woman appears to have been literally fornicated into an insane frenzy. It appears that she was rammed with an object so forcefully and continuously that she bled from the force of it, but what a smile she had on her face, as if she had actually seen heaven."

Chablis offered some explanation. "You will think us crazy I suppose, but we were following the perpetrator of this crime?"

"Oh, you were, and who are you may I ask?"

"I am Chablis Louise Chavez, Private Detective from New York City, in service to my friend here, Carlton Broughton. As I said, we have been trailing the perpetrator."

CHABLIS AND THE DILDO FROM HELL

The captain, licking his upper teeth and making a smacking sound, said "OK, so tell me all about it."

"You wouldn't believe it Captain. I am not even sure I believe it."

"Try me."

"O.K., you asked for it. There is a wild dildo on the lose."

The captain and his officer burst out in uncontrollable laughter, as Chablis and Carlton stood stoic and serious, not cracking even the slightest smile. The two of them together laid out the details of the Karson invention and all the years of misery it had caused. The captain, after politely listening to them said, "Well, of course, we have all heard rumours over the years, but in all honesty I am afraid we cannot lend much credence to the existence of a frenzied dildo that fornicates victims to near death. The woman was obviously ravaged with a large object most likely similar to a dildo and the assault was conducted in an incredibly violent way. The crime is less than two hours old at this point. We have not moved her yet, because we are waiting for the helicopter from Brattleboro General to arrive, so she can be transported there. I am one hundred percent sure they will discount any evidence that would point to a fornicating mad dildo as the culprit."

CHABLIS AND THE DILDO FROM HELL

"Captain," said a determinedly serious Carlton, "they can discount whatever they want. We followed the damn thing for many hours as it was no more than perhaps three hours in front of us, and obviously, its first action on making shore here in the village was to find a victim upon whom it could unleash its fury. You have a serial fucker on the lose that will lay waste to men and women alike, and God-forbid, maybe even children. This thing is capable of abominations you would not believe. It has proven it again and again over many years. It is in a fornicating frenzy now, because it feels it has been abysmally wronged and hell knows no evil worse than a dildo that feels it has been wronged."

Again, the captain and officer burst out in nearly uncontrollable laughter, as Chablis added: "Laugh your fucking heads off. At one time I would have joined you, but I have conversed with the damn thing. I spent nearly two hours listening to its tales of woe. It feels it has been wronged and it is on a path of destruction."

The two men were now almost bending over with laughter as the captain managed to say, "You two can go, but stay close by. There is only a B & B here. Mrs. Ames," he pointed to his right, "right down Main Street to Cloverdale. Left on Cloverdale and it is the third house on the right. Huge yellow Victorian. You can't miss it," he said as his chortling continued.

CHABLIS AND THE DILDO FROM HELL

Chablis and Carlton, shaking their heads in unison, walked out without another word. As they walked toward the Bed and Breakfast, Chablis instinctively surveyed the surroundings to scrutinize any place where Dandy might be hiding, waiting for his next victim. The house was a well-kept mansion from the turn of the 20th century and Mrs. Ames was an amiable host who ushered them to a third floor bedroom that was decorated tastefully with antiques from the early 1900's.

Chablis walked over to the large bay window in a torrent, sighed, looked out onto Cloverdale Street and said, "There is a wild, unrestrained dildo out there somewhere, and we are the only two who know the truth about it."

They were called in by a state investigator who had showed up and they were basically dismissed as a couple of kooks. The attack was indeed the result of a wild frenzy of a fuck that almost ripped the woman apart, and the investigator did say that it was likely the woman had an incredibly wild orgasm as she was still babbling about what a grand fuck it was. Chablis and Carlton left the station again shaking their heads, unable to get anyone to listen to what they knew. The fact that Chablis was a well-known investigator seemed to carry no weight. The two of them had dinner at a restaurant on Main Street where whispers could be heard as apparently rumours of their explanation of the attack had spread.

CHABLIS AND THE DILDO FROM HELL

As the two were walking back in the twilight of the day they passed a park on Main Street when suddenly they heard a shrill and dreadful cry. Chablis could feel the blood trickling in her veins and tingling in the extremities of her limbs so loud was the scream, but there was something unusual about it, something one would not connect to fear. There was a tinge of ecstasy to the scream. This state lasted but for an instant; the scream was repeated, and they rushed in the direction from whence it came. There on the park bench was a sighing creature with a broad smile on her face, thrown across the bench, her head hanging down and her pale and distorted features half covered by her hair. Her dress was pulled up around her waist and semen was streaming from her vagina that was grotesquely stretched. Chablis asked the lady if she was O.K. and only got a deep sigh of satisfaction from her. Obviously, the woman was in a blissful state and needed no consoling.

Chablis glanced to her right and signalled they should head into the brush, because Dandy had to be nearby. As they rushed out the back side of the park, they saw it. Rapidly rolling down the street was a fiendish figure that had just committed a heinous act of fornicating another woman into blissfulness. Drawing her pistol, Chablis was about to fire when Dandy leaped to his right and bounded into a nearby forest with the swiftness of lightning. They pursued him, but as they got to the shores of the lake, Dandy dived in and sank beneath the waves and darkness was now engulfing the area. The two bowed their heads and spent the rest of the night eliciting laughter again as the only response to their pleas for some understanding, as the new victim could only babble incoherently about being fucked by a wild fornicator who delivered an orgasm for the ages.

The two women who had experienced the wrath of Dandy were transported by helicopter to the Brattleboro hospital, where, they would, no doubt, be put in a psych ward and evaluated for hallucinatory drugs.

As she lay naked beside Carlton, Chablis suddenly jerked herself up. As Carlton slowly sat up, Chablis looked out the window where the wind was whirring about, and the rain fell in torrents. It was almost morning, and Chablis shouted, "Fuck. He is gone. Come, we must sail back across the lake."

Bewildered, but seeing she was not to be denied, Carlton went with her to their stolen boat and the two began, in the pouring rain to make their way back across the lake. Chablis was in deep thought and Carlton respected her introspection with silence. Chablis' eyes were trained on the far shore. The rain had ceased, and the curse of Dandy had simply gone on too long. An end had to be at hand. This abomination of fornicating madness had to be stopped.

CHABLIS AND THE DILDO FROM HELL

As they made their way to shore, clouds formed in the sky and darkness pressed upon them. Chablis reflected on her youth, when she would wander about in flowery meadows and pleasant vales with friends, but she was often in a dungeon of despair in her youth because of her gender dysphasia. No one in the little Mexican village where the church told her she was an abomination could understand her, not even her parents, save one lone soul, the manager of the factory where she worked. He befriended her and they became lovers. He was her salvation, and then she knew instinctively that Dandy, having assumed he had thrown them off the track, was in search of his salvation.

Yes, Dandy was in search of that most elusive commodity – liberty, freedom to just be left alone to enjoy life. Liberty, however, was a fiction for Americans, who did not realize the invisible chains that kept them imprisoned to a bankrupt idea of exceptionalism that was non-existent. The government and its corporate masters kept selling an idea to keep the masses at bay, and even Dandy was a victim. It was not Dandy that was the monster. It was society at large. Chablis began to reflect on past misfortunes and saw that the real monster was a society that had no core, a nation that was founded on a lie and on hypocrisy. No, the monster was not Dandy at all, but the society that spawned the ill treatment of all that dared to be different.

CHABLIS AND THE DILDO FROM HELL

Yes, Dandy was paying for his difference as all who were different did. Fit the mould or be a pariah. She looked over at Carlton, and she realized his cause was flawed. He was possessed by a maddening rage when he thought of what happened to his mother and father, and desired and ardently wanted Dandy within his grasp to wreak a great and single revenge on his cursed mushroom head.

It was at that very moment that Chablis realized she could not pursue Dandy Dildo with the idea of punishment. She saw in Carlton a rage for revenge of a perceived wrong, which was, in reality, mere circumstance.

She trembled with excess of agitation as she said. "There is frenzy in your manner, and something, I doubt not, of that haughty fierceness which the martyrs of old are said to have possessed. But I say to you that you must temper your rage."

"What?" he cried. "I dare you to question my veracity of purpose. This entity destroyed the love of my mother and father."

"No, Dandy Dildo was just what came between them at the time. Had it not been he, it would have been something else. You carry a grudge with no basis in fact. Let go of your hatred or it will destroy you."

CHABLIS AND THE DILDO FROM HELL

CHAPTER 12
THE LAST IMPEDIMENT HAD DIED

The sun was glistening on his balls
as he strolled to hope's gate.
For he had many peccadilloes,
and many a tete-a-tete.
For someone most salacious
clothed only in bare skin,
did he really belong there,
where some wanted him in.

Upon arriving, Dandy Dildo
was escorted to the din.
He was a lively rousing dildo
amid bounteous sweaty skin.
Women wanted his throbbing piece,
unto the breach went thrusting in,
and to joy he could find no purchase
in that mountainous wall of skin.

For there were buttocks for an altar

CHABLIS AND THE DILDO FROM HELL

and virgins at the stake,
and with a Venus in a truss
so much more than he could take.
So much more than he could take,
so much more than he could break –
where the buttocks made an altar,
and the virgins were at stake.

And he gave himself to pleasure
and lost himself in what was called sin,
and set about with purpose
of breaking in some skin.
From alabaster Grecian tones,
to the deepest midnight black,
such that longing by himself
would never get what he wanted back.

For has it not been prophesied
by masters long ago:
'Within the walls of Sodom,
any man may go?
And as he found himself staggering through
Corinthians grandest galore,
he wondered for dissolution
with yet another whore.

For there were fannies in the cloister
and maidens on the make,
and beggars on their bellies,
so much more than he could take,
so much more than he could take.
So much more than could break –

J. Wayne Frye

CHABLIS AND THE DILDO FROM HELL

with fannies in the cloister
and maidens on the make.

Exhausted, he lay back upon
the silk upholstered pew,
sighing heavily was he,
gazing upon the vision anew.
To such a deep delight 'twould win him,
all this writhing in the end,
this music of the fleshly spheres,
this orchestra of skin.

But as he stood, once more prepared,
to enter into the fray,
it seemed that his libido
had nothing more to say.
For therein lies the rub,
when all the rubbing's done -
flesh must meet the reaper once,
for Felecia his song was now sung.

Chablis had fit the final piece of the puzzle together, but she feared sharing it with Carlton, as he harboured so much hatred. All voluntary thought was swallowed up and lost. She saw Carlton was hurried away by fury; revenge alone endowed him with strength and composure; it moulded his feelings and allowed him to be calculating and calm with determination to finally wrought havoc upon what he saw as an evil entity that had come between the two people he loved most in the world.

CHABLIS AND THE DILDO FROM HELL

Carlton asked her by what clue they might trace the steps of their fiendish enemy. But her plan was unsettled, and she wandered how to calm him and let him see the light of compassion. As night approached they were at the ruins where it all had seemingly begun. The place seemed to cast a dark shadow, which was felt but not seen. There was grief here, but also rage and despair. Yet, within Chablis the rage had subsided as she knew that even a lowly dildo with human characteristics deserved peace. But how could she get Carlton to understand that?

She reached down and took Carlton's hand. "The spirits of the dead, are wandering here and you my dear are a minister of vengeance, to aid and conduct that which you think a holy act of retribution. That cursed and hellish monster has drunk now for many, many years from a cup of agony; he has felt the torment of despair. He has lived a hellish existence."

She was answered through the stillness of night by a loud and fiendish laugh. It rang on her ears long and heavily; the mountains re-echoed it, and she felt as if all hell surrounded her with mockery and laughter. This was the laugh of vengeance. The laughter died away, when Carlton whispered, "I am an unsatisfied, miserable wretch! You have determined to let it live, and I am not satisfied. You were to ease my pain by making it possible for me to destroy that thing."

CHABLIS AND THE DILDO FROM HELL

"You are destroying yourself Carlton, not that damn dildo."

"Hogwash."

"Carlton, you are a good and decent man who has simply let the desire to minister revenge for a perceived wrong rule your life for far too long now."

"You know something, Chablis. I can see it in your damn eyes. You know where that hellacious monster is. I must destroy that abomination. I must! He is the enemy of love. I must wrestle it for my sanity. I vow vengeance to torture it as it tortured my mom and dad. Never will I give up my search until he or I perish; and then with what ecstasy shall I say it is finished between it and me."

Chablis lowered her head and said, "I know where he hides, and he is waiting for us. He is tired of running. He took us on one last journey in hopes that we would give up when we saw the destruction of which he was capable, but as he sank below the water leaving us on the shore, I knew that he had seen we were unrepentant in our determination, in our pursuit, so he awaits us now. How he waits I do not know whether it is with furious intentions or with the quiet resignation to his fate – an end to his agonies, a termination of the misery that has been his life."

CHABLIS AND THE DILDO FROM HELL

Carlton was undeterred in his hatred. "Despair has ruled my life, ruled my father's life." Still, he harboured compassion at the same time, because he saw the goodness in Chablis. "That night in the study with my father you gave him the one real stroke in remembrance of the glory of his love for my mother. He had many women over the years, but as I hid behind a curtain by the vestibule in the hallway that night, I saw tears in his eyes as he ascended the stairs. You gave him a grand moment, the one moment in fifty years of true remembrance Chablis. Yours was the blow job that took him to heaven for a few minutes as he remembered the glory of the love he had for my mother. You are a woman of infinite compassion. Most people cannot understand the sanctity of something as simple as a blow job, but you are wise far beyond any woman I have ever known. You must take me to Dandy Dildo for if I do not face him I shall harbour this misery deep within me for all eternity." Tears were now streaming down his cheeks. "It is my destiny. It is Dandy's destiny that we come face-to-face and end our torment once and for all."

Despair had indeed thrown the Broughton family asunder, and they had sunk beneath the muck of misery. Maybe it was indeed fitting that Chablis bring them face-to-face.

Thus, the two began the journey to Dandy, for Chablis knew where he was, where his only hope for love lay. The journey would be on foot and it would be long and arduous. It was more than a physical journey. It was a journey of the soul, as Carlton had to finally put his hatred to rest.

They traversed the valley, climbing a large hill and stood at its summit viewing the expanse before them with anguish of heart, mind, body and soul, when suddenly Chablis' eye caught a dark speck upon the dusky plain ahead. It was smoke coming from a cottage in the far distance. She strained her sight to discover the fertile valley that lay ahead and thought of what must have transpired between Dandy and the woman he loved, who was the only women who genuinely loved him for more than his sexual prowess.

Warm tears filled her eyes, which she hastily wiped away, but still her sight was dimmed by the burning drops, until, giving way to the emotions that oppressed her, she wept within for the pain that Dandy, Carlton and his father had endured all because a man named Karson had so loved his wife that he wanted to give her the ultimate orgasm. Who could have known the pain and agony wrought from a simple act of love, but that act had led to egregious harm, because the devoted man-servant, Harold, had less than honourable intentions and went to the extreme to procure parts for Dandy that had ultimately led to his own demise in a furious butt-fucking on the laboratory table where Dandy was born.

CHABLIS AND THE DILDO FROM HELL

Chablis looked at a determined Carlton as he now appeared almost within grasp of his foe. As if by evil omen, the sky became cloudy and darkness swelled about them as thunder rumbled in the distance. The wind arose; the rain came down as if being poured from buckets; and, as with the mighty shock of an earthquake, the roaring thunder split and cracked with a tremendous and overwhelming clamour. Was this the Gods of Fate causing a tumultuous uproar to keep them from their perceived enemy? In this manner many appalling minutes passed, until finally the clamour and rain slowed.

They made their way through a graveyard and Chablis noticed that there was one grave there that was fairly fresh, the earth still piled loosely upon it. There was a simple wooden marker on the grave and the name seemed to jump out and vibrate within Chablis' mind. It bore the name of Felicia's father. The last impediment to the union of Dandy and Felicia had died.

J. Wayne Frye

EPILOGUE
THE LIGHT OF HOPE FLICKERED

Be ye not condemned.
Each day look
Upon the horizon of hope.

Chablis looked to her left at the countenance of Carlton and could see his eyes were now lighted up with indignation, now subdued to downcast sorrow and quenched in infinite wretchedness. His agitation was like a volcano bursting forth, his face had an expression of the wildest rage imaginable. She asked herself why she was allowing this to happen. How could she end the happiness that she knew Dandy had finally found in the arms of Felicia? Yes, he had fled to her in hopes that she would offer him the warmth of her love by the hearth of hope in that little cottage. To Dandy, that simple humble place was a pantheon of light in a world of increasing darkness that was slowly claiming his soul.

CHABLIS AND THE DILDO FROM HELL

Chablis reached over and placed her left hand on Carlton's right arm as they raced forward toward the cabin. "Are you on the verge of madness my friend? Where does this endless pursuit of that which you deem the paramount evil lead you? We all create demoniacal enemies when the real enemy is within us – the enemy is often ourselves. Are you sure that your enemy my dear Carlton is not yourself? I have pursued this thing I thought an abomination, a thing that I thought was a figment of people's imagination, and it may well be a figment of all our imaginations, because we all harbour enemies within, because life is a frightful prospect for all but the few. Day in and day out we toil in obscurity for the miniscule rewards that come to us, but what is the meaning of it all? People seek out religion because they want to believe that this abysmal thing called life is not all there is. They are desperate to believe there is something better, something worthwhile after this life. Truth is – there is nothing – this is it, Carlton. We – you – need to make this life worthwhile, and letting hatred overwhelm you is destroying the chance you have for happiness. Dandy came here to this lonely, desolate place because this is the only place where he can find happiness and love."

"Chablis, the only joy that I can now know will be when my shattered spirit puts that thing to death. Can you not somehow understand my anguish?"

CHABLIS AND THE DILDO FROM HELL

"I understand your anguish, your pain, your heartache. I also understand his, Carlton. My darling man, the way of life is not smooth, and that which occurs in our childhood forever abides within us for good or ill. We must face dangers and terror, because at every new incident your fortitude has to be called forth and your courage exhibited, because danger and death surrounded us on a daily basis."

They made their way to the cabin, where only the light of the fireplace flickered. Sighing heavily, Carlton stopped by the window. They both looked in and observed Felicia sitting in a rocker by the fireplace with Dandy in her lap. She was gently stroking him as the two were in connubial bliss. Carlton turned to Chablis and said, "Your incredible beauty shines through the bleakness and despair, and you glow like an angel of light in the darkness. I often find myself overwhelmed with the blackness of despair, but you are a beacon of hope that forever shines on a path to Nirvana."

Chablis smiled at him and they listened as Dandy said to Felicia, "With you I am safe. You are the angel that opens the gates to my heaven in your arms. I was drowning in a sea of misery and you threw me the life-jacket of love that buoyed me upward into your outstretched arms. You embraced me with love and made me whole. You were the lifeguard of love who gave me hope

CHABLIS AND THE DILDO FROM HELL

when I had none. You my sweetheart resuscitated me with your love. You breathed hope into a hopeless thing. You shined a light on me that lifted me from the dark waters that were about to pull me under for the last time."

Out of the night that covered me,
Black as the pit from pole to pole,
I thank whatever spirits may be
For my unconquerable soul.

In the fell clutch of circumstance
I have not winced nor cried aloud.
Under the bludgeonings of chance
My head is bloody, but unbowed.

Beyond this place of wrath and tears
Looms but the horror of the shade,
And yet the menace of the years
Finds and shall find me unafraid.

It matters not how strait the gate,
How charged with punishments the scroll,
I am the master of my fate,
I am the captain of my soul.

Chablis and Carlton, holding hands, walked away from the cabin where the light of hope flickered in the darkness for Felicia and Dandy.

THE END

J. Wayne Frye

**MORE
CHABLIS LOUISE CHAVEZ
MYSTERIES
FROM
FIRESIDE BOOKS**

Chablis: Avenging Angel for the Forgotten
In the City of Lost Hope
Chablis and the Terrorist Who Resurrected the Spirit of Che
Pursuit
The Disappearance